A LAKE SERIES NOVELLA

By

AnnaLisa Grant

ISBN-13:978-1511666169
ISBN-10:1511666161

Table of Contents

Chapter 1

"I will never understand how something so small and utterly adorable can make such a huge and foul-smelling mess in her diaper!" I hear Will coo from across the hall in the nursery. The sun is just rising and so are the twins, a gift from them in the last few days. They're four months old now and finally sleeping for longer stretches after their last feeding.

I stretch my tired body and roll out of bed, tying my hair back in a ponytail as I shuffle my way to meet Will and help. The twins have started the stage where they grab at everything and I've suffered enough baby death grips to my hair to have learned to keep it out of their way.

Before I walk into the nursery, I stand in the doorway for a moment and just watch him. From day one, Will has been the most amazing father. He's never baulked at changing a dirty diaper, and he got up with me every time when the babies were still feeding twice a night. And while those are awesome and super helpful things, my favorite thing about Will being a dad is watching the way he looks at our girls. There is this amazing light in his eyes. He is so in love with them that he can't help but beam.

There was a time when he thought he was going to have to try really hard not to be like his father, distant and unloving, but I've known from the very start that Will doesn't have an uncaring molecule in his body. His love and care for the girls has been as natural to him as breathing.

"It's adorable poop, though, right?" I say as I enter the room.

"Our girls are cute, but they do not poop rainbows and glitter." Will finishes fastening Natalie's diaper and kisses her on the head as he lifts her to him. Then he kisses me on the forehead and smiles. "They're both done. You can go back to bed if you want."

"That's sweet, but you need me to at least get you set up with both of them and two bottles. I'm happy to be up." I kiss Natalie and cross the nursery to pick up my sweet baby Claire.

When we found out I was carrying two girls I thought Will was going to faint … and then go out and buy an arsenal of guns. Once he recovered, he was swift to suggest we keep the original girl name we had, Natalie Eliana, and name Baby B after my two mothers: Claire Elizabeth. He said we'd just have to keep trying for a boy so we could use the boy name we had picked out: Andrew Luke.

With the help of our mothers, we've been able to establish and stay in a pretty good routine with the girls. It was really hard at first, but with so much help it's been as smooth a transition a new mom could ever hope for. And even though I don't need them nearly as much as I did in the beginning, Mom and Eliana still find their way over to the house a couple of times a week.

"Are you going into the office today? You know you have to go back at some point," I say to Will. He's basically been running the company from his phone for the last four months, only going in when I begged him to get out of the house before we killed each other. It's hard to tear him away from the two little girls who have him wrapped around their little fingers already.

"I hadn't planned on it. Jeremy has been holding down the fort pretty well. I think I'll be going back next week, though. I'm actually looking forward to spending a long day at work and then coming home to the beautiful faces of all three of my girls." Will leans in and kisses me sweetly. I love that his kisses still make my heart flutter.

"That'll be nice," I say. "I'm having lunch with our moms today, but I'm going to run out a bit longer, if that's okay with you."

"That's great. You need to start getting out more, too, you know."

"Yes, yes, I know," I agree.

We get the girls settled in their bouncy seats after they eat and tag-team on showering. It takes me almost an hour to figure out what I'm going to wear. Well, more like what I'm able to wear. The skinny jeans I once slid into easily aren't exactly my best friend right now. Eliana keeps telling me I need to give myself a little time. "Pregnancy changes us, dear," she says.

"You look great, babe," Will tells me as I emerge from the closet.

"Looks like I'm going to need a couple of pairs of jeans that don't cut off my circulation, at least until I'm back to my pre-twins body." I twist my mouth and give a disappointed sigh.

"Hey..." Will pulls me to him and kisses me. "I won't pretend to understand how you're feeling, but just know that I could care less. I think you look amazing!"

"Thanks. You're sweet. I might be calling on Wes to give me some Marine training though. I'm pretty sure if anyone can kick my butt into gear, it's Wesley Furtick!" I laugh.

"Don't let him kick it too much. I'm kind of loving your post-baby butt." Will slides his hands from my waist to my backside and gives me a little squeeze as he kisses my neck.

"Will!" I squeal.

"Come on, babe," he mumbles into my neck as he continues kissing me.

"Hey!" I say as I pretend to push him off me. "We agreed we weren't going to be weird and do stuff with the babies in the room." We both look over at our girls sleeping peacefully in their seats.

Will gives me one last hard kiss on the lips and pulls himself away. "Fine, but we are picking up where we left off tonight!"

"I'm good with that," I say with a little bite of my lip.

"That is unfair." Will raises an eyebrow at me and I just walk away with a smirk.

A little something to eat and an hour of snuggling with my baby girls later, I finally get myself together to leave. Will makes me promise to take my time and enjoy my "me" time, especially since I'm about to be home alone with two babies who are getting bigger every day. Before we know it they'll be scooting and crawling along the floor, and we'll be forced to put a safety gate up and throw them in baby jail.

I wish lunch with Mom and Eliana was *just* a lunch. I have something important to talk with them about. Normally I would go to Will, but I'm not sure if it's a good idea just yet. I don't want to upset him, and I think that maybe I can just handle it on my own. If I tell Will, he's going to move in a direction that I have a sinking feeling will end up breaking his heart.

I drive down our beautiful, tree-lined street and approach Caroline's house. Well, her parents' house. Caroline partnered with an amazing interior designer a couple of years ago and divides her time between California and New York because that's what he does. I don't get to see her as often as I'd like, but we do our best to stay in touch. She did come in town when Natalie and Claire were born, which was pretty special.

I'm about to drive by when I see Mrs. Jackson's car in their driveway. She's usually not home this time of day, so I decide to pop in and see her. I've been meaning to chat with her about volunteer opportunities at Community Support, the agency she started last year when she got tired of the hospital scene. They serve families and individuals with needs ranging from housing to clothing to food. They also offer free counseling and parenting classes. With a generous donation from Weston, Fincher, and Marks, as well as Heyward Prep, the agency is well prepared to run for several years while they build up even more community sponsors.

I ring the doorbell and wait patiently for someone to answer. The Jacksons' home is just as big as ours, and getting to the door before your guest gives up and leaves can sometimes be a test of wills. The door opens and Suzanne, Mrs. Jackson's housekeeper, answers.

"Hi Layla! How are you, darlin'?" she asked in her sweet southern voice.

"I'm great! Thanks, Suzanne. How are you?"

"I'm as happy as a raccoon on trash day!" She giggles.

"That's awesome," I say, laughing. Suzanne opens the door wider as I cross the threshold.

"C'mon, darlin'. They're in the back."

They are in the back? Puzzled, I follow Suzanne to the back porch.

When I see them sitting there I can't decide if I'm happy or furious.

My brow furrows in confusion at the sight. There, sitting on the loveseat glider, are Caroline and Tyler, holding hands while Tyler nuzzles Caroline's neck.

"Caroline? Tyler?"

"Layla!" Caroline says as she stands up, seemingly just as shocked as I am. "What are you doing here?"

"I was just about to ask you the same thing. Aren't you supposed to be in New York or Los Angeles right now? And, uh … how long has *this* been going on?" I fold my arms in front of me and wait for her reply.

"Well … um," she begins with a stutter. "I'm only in town for a few days and I know you're super busy with the babies and Tyler was able squeeze a couple of days off last minute and … Ty?"

I raise my eyebrows and cock my head to the side in anticipation of Tyler's fumbled response.

"Well … It's been six months," he says, answering the most important of my questions.

"Six months!"

"Before you freak out," Caroline begins.

"Too late! How could you keep this from me?" I've got a rush of mixed emotions swirling in me. I'm thrilled for Caroline and Tyler but I'm hurt that she never told me she was even interested in him. We've always shared everything with each other.

"Just listen, Layla. It all started very suddenly when Ty came out to California on business. We had dinner and before we knew it we were watching the sunrise from the roof of my apartment building. I wanted to tell you, but you were so close to having the twins that I thought I'd just fill you in when I came to see the babies. Then, well, I got here and I didn't want to make it about me."

I thought for a minute, trying to put myself in Caroline's shoes. If something as monumental as having a baby was happening in Caroline's life, I probably would have done the same thing. I wouldn't have wanted to take any of the attention off her.

"Well … I guess I can understand that. But no more secrets, okay?" I smile and shake my head in disbelief that my two best friends are together. "Just wait until I tell Will!"

"He, uh, kind of already knows," Tyler stammers.

"What? I'm going to take back my forgiveness of you. Why would you tell him and not me? And why wouldn't he tell me?"

"He wanted to tell you but I wouldn't let him. I wanted to be the one to tell you," Caroline explains. "You've been so busy with the babies like you should be. I just … somehow it never seemed to be the right time." Caroline looks down, looking sad, like she lost her best friend to two people who poop in their pants and drool.

"Hey," I say as I approach her. "Being a mom has turned my life upside down and changed me in ways I never knew were possible, but none of it changes how important you are to me. Please don't ever feel like you can't come to me, talk to me, like you used to. You may have to hold and feed a baby while you talk, but I'm always here for you."

"I know. And I'm sorry that I didn't tell you sooner. Trust me, there were times when I was dying to tell you. I was just trying to be understanding about everything you had going on. And I will hold one of those adorable little girls any day of the week! Especially if it means getting to spend time with you when I'm in town."

"Well, either I was completely oblivious, or you two did an amazing job hiding this from me when you were both here over a month ago!" I chuckle.

"Oh, honey, you were so out of it!" Caroline laughs.

"Newborn-induced sleep deprivation will do that to you!"

"For the record, I told her she should tell you a long time ago," Tyler says in his defense as he draws the two of us to his side.

"I'll give you half credit for effort," I tease. "Does Will know you're in town, Care?"

"Nah. It really was all last minute," Tyler begins. "Caroline ended up with a few days off and I was able to rearrange some meetings at the bank so I could see her. I'm supposed to go to New York in a couple of weeks when she's there, so this is bonus time." Tyler smiles brighter than I've ever seen him smile as he kisses Caroline on the temple. That's all it takes for me to know that their relationship isn't going to be a flash in the pan. This is real and I have a feeling I'll be picking out bridesmaid dresses with Caroline before I know it.

"So, you didn't come over just to bust us. What's up?" Caroline asks.

"Oh, your mom and I are working on a new initiative at the agency. Just thought I'd stop by and touch base with her on it. I mean, now that the girls are sleeping well both at night and during the day," I tell her.

"Nothing like a good night's sleep to make you feel like you can take on the world!" Mrs. Jackson says as she descends the staircase next to us.

"I know, right, Mrs. Jackson!" I agree.

"Just as long as you're not going to do too much, Layla. You want to be sure to take time for yourself while those little ones are napping. Especially when they start getting mobile here in a few months. They'll be scooting all over the place before you know it! And please, Layla, we've worked together enough for you to call me Carol. You're not in high school anymore." She cocks her head to the side and gives me a look that reminds me of just how many times she's told me this.

Mrs. Jackson—Carol—and I have worked closely together over the last few years as she was quite connected to the agency where I was working before the twins came. She did some contract counseling with some of our more emotionally scarred clients, many of whom were like me: present when their parents died. And, of course, I worked closely with Carol as she started her own agency.

"Yes, of course … Carol." I smile apologetically with a telekinetic promise to try to remember next time. "Really, this *will* be me time. I'm four months in and, even though Will has been home seventy-five percent of the time, I fully recognize my need for adult conversation. I asked mom to read off her grocery list to me last week, so, yeah."

That probably sounded worse than it was, but that was an especially hard day. While Will has usually just gone into the office for a couple of hours after the girls ate, he ended up being gone all day. Six hours. I managed fine with the twins on my own, but I hadn't realized until then just how much I valued speaking in complete, coherent sentences.

"I know it's been twenty-five years, but I haven't forgotten those days!" Carol laughs. "Well, I'm sure we can come up with a schedule that works well for you. I'd love to chat with you more, but we're about to head out. I see that you've stumbled upon our little secret here. I'm so glad! It was exhausting keeping this from you!"

"Yes, she's in the know now, mother. Layla has forgiven us, so let's not remind her of how in the dark she was!" Caroline gently shoves her mother toward the foyer table so she can retrieve her purse, with Carol laughing out her protest with every step.

"All right! All right!" Carol relents. "Can we talk next week, Layla?"

"Of course! I was just on my way to do some shopping and meet the moms for lunch. I'll be around next week, so just let me know when is good for you!" I adjust the strap of my purse across my body and move toward the door. "Now that I know, please come over and see me … both of you! Maybe dinner before you have to go back to L.A.?"

"Definitely!" Caroline says as she hugs my neck. It makes me miss her. She's in such high demand now that she's decorated the homes of some of Hollywood's hottest. She hardly ever gets to come home to visit, and I guess when she has, she's come to see Tyler.

We all exit at the same time, hugging before I split from them. I watch the three of them file into Carol's car as I click my seatbelt into place.

"Caroline and Tyler," I say with a sigh. It really is wonderful. Perfect, really. I shake my head, thinking of what else awaits me today. What isn't perfect is the conversation I'm about to have with Mom and Eliana.

Chapter 2

I pass through the second turn-about on my way to meet Mom and Eliana for lunch. We're meeting at Campania, the same place Will and I had our wedding reception. Until the babies were born we tried to meet once a week. Since then, the moms have occasionally brought lunch or dinner over, and a couple of times they had Vinnie put together a sampler of my and Will's favorites.

Walking in, I'm greeting by the same warm atmosphere I always have, and I'm reminded of just how much I love this place. I remember the first time Will brought me here after our Day of Nothing. It was a stressful time in our lives, but the journey was worth the destination.

Mom and Eliana are already seated when I pass through the velvet-curtained doorway but jump to their feet when they see me. Their faces shine brightly with joy as they extend their arms to hug me. They don't even wait for me to meet them at the table. I'm quickly accosted in the middle of the room. Fortunately there are only four other parties dining during this non-rush hour in the middle of the week, all of whom are seated on the other side of the room.

"Layla, honey, you look wonderful!" Mom says as her arms wrap tightly around me.

"Yes! Just beautiful!" Eliana agrees.

"Bathing will do that for you." I laugh as I hug them both fiercely. We sit and our server, Stacey, immediately brings me a diet cola with limes. "Oh, I love you!" I say to all three of them. I take a long draw through the straw and sigh.

"Are you all ready or do you need a few minutes?" she asks.

"I'm going to need a minute, if that's okay?" I tell her.

"Sure. I'll be back in a few!"

I peruse the menu as if I've never seen it before. I don't want to miss it if Vinnie has added something to his repertoire. After a first run down the page, I realize it wouldn't matter anyway because all I want is a Caprese Panini with a spring salad.

"That's what you get every time!" Mom teases.

"I know, but it's just so good!" I laugh.

Stacey takes our orders and we adjust in our seats as we settle in to wait for our meals to be made fresh.

"We have gifts!" Eliana says, dragging two gift bags from their hiding place under the table. Each bag is identical, as I'm anticipating the gifts inside will be.

"You really shouldn't have! As if you all didn't already go overboard with them at Christmas, and they were only six weeks old! The girls can't even sit up yet and they're already better dressed than I ever have been! They are so spoiled!" I pull the tissue paper out of the bag and fold it neatly. I've got quite a stash of tissue paper and gift bags stored away in my closet to use for future gifts for the girls.

I unwrap the tissue and find the most ridiculously adorable tights with ruffles on the bottom and the tiniest pairs of black patent shoes. We give a collective "aww" and I smile from ear to ear. The next bag has two dresses that are certain to make Natalie and Claire look like princesses. I'm pleasantly surprised to find that one is pink and one is white. I know they don't have a clue right now, but I want to try and avoid matching every single outfit they wear. It will be important for them to have their own identity.

"You two really are too much! Thank you!" I say with a broad smile.

"They're size six months so they'll have time to grow into them. Are they still in zero to three months?" Eliana asks.

As we expected, the twins were early and therefore pretty tiny when they were born. Natalie was five pounds, two ounces, and Claire was five pounds, four ounces. Good sizes for twins born at thirty six weeks, but still so small.

"Mostly, but I've started pulling out a few three to six months. They seem to swim in them, but they'll get there. Thank you, again." I pack the gifts back into one bag and put all the folded tissue in the other and set them next to me on the floor. When I sit up there is a small square box sitting on the table before me. Mom and Eliana are wearing face-splitting grins. I cock a suspicious eye up and immediately refuse the gift.

"The girls do not need jewelry, too! I know you love them, but really, moms, I have to draw the line somewhere." I say it as sugary sweet as I can. I don't want to hurt their feelings but there has to be a limit. I figured I should set it now while the girls have no clue. If I wait until they're aware, Will and I will be in big trouble.

"It's not for the girls. It's for you." Mom smiles that sweet, Claire smile of hers, making me want to cry even before I see what it is.

I pull the small, velvet jewelry box out of the slightly larger box it is nestled in and creak the top open. With my free hand I cover my mouth in shock while tears fill my eyes and overflow.

"Oh, mom," I breathe out only slightly above a whisper. Cushioned inside the box is a necklace almost identical to the one I gave Claire our first Christmas together. Strung neatly on the silver chain are four beads, each representing my own little family by our birthstones: topaz for Natalie & Claire, alexandrite for me, and tanzanite for Will.

I want to speak, but my heart is in my throat and I can't seem to catch my breath. I am completely and utterly overwhelmed.

"I … this is," I begin but the words get tangled up in my effort to keep from bawling right there in the middle of the restaurant. So I stand and round the table where Claire stands to meet me. My arms wrap around her like a vice. I bury my face into her neck and let out a few sobs of pure joy before composing myself enough to speak.

"I love it, Mom. Thank you so much."

"Now you have an idea of what I felt that Christmas morning." She moves her collar and reveals the necklace I gave her all those years ago now. Luke has added more beads over the years, but centered among all of them are the birthstone charms I started the piece with.

Eliana wipes the tears that have fallen from her eyes as she smiles at us brightly.

"There was a time my tears would have been from a place of sadness for thinking I would go the rest of my life without having what your family has, Claire. Who would have thought I would get to be a part of it one day? Now my tears are from utter joy," Eliana says before she hugs us.

The three of us stand there in a group hug and I can't help but giggle at how silly we must look to the restaurant patrons. It makes me so happy to see how far Eliana has come since I met her. Her relationship with Wes has been wonderful for her personal growth. She's strong now and readily expresses her feelings … all of them!

We take our places at the table just in time as Stacey approaches with our lunches. And before I can ask, Stacey takes my empty glass and tells me she'll return with a new drink in a minute.

"So, Layla, you said you had something you wanted to talk to us about. Is everything okay?" Mom asks before she takes the first bite of her salad.

I look at both her and Eliana and twist my mouth to the side, considering where to start. It was just a few days ago when Rachel Meadows came to see me. I had no idea who she was from her name alone. But when she told me Michael Meadows, Will's brother, was her husband, my heart raced.

The last—and only—time we saw Michael, he made it abundantly clear that he was not interested in developing a relationship with Will. He said his piece and walked out of our lives. We had heard from his mother Victoria that he got married, but it was really just a passing comment one time when we had Will's extended family over for dinner a few years ago. It's been a process, but we've come to have a really good relationship with Will's half-siblings and their mothers. Some are closer than others, but it's all wonderful.

Rachel must have been watching the house to wait for Will to leave that day because no sooner had he pulled out of the driveway than Rachel was ringing the doorbell. I invited her in, and after I poured her a cup of coffee she explained why she had come to see me.

"Michael is sick," she began. "Really sick."

"I'm so sorry. Do they know what's wrong?"

"He has cancer. Pancreatic cancer." My heart sank as she moved her coffee from one hand to the other and then back again. I couldn't imagine facing that with Will.

"Oh, Rachel. I'm so sorry." I didn't really know what to say. I didn't know this woman at all and there she was, sitting in my living room, telling me that her husband had cancer and was going to die.

"Can I ask why you're here telling me this?" I posed.

"Well, first off, Michael doesn't know I'm here. In fact, I think he'd be pretty upset if he knew. He even swore his mother to secrecy because I think he knew she'd tell Will," she said. "But, um … the hospital bills …"

My heart sank even further to find out that she was only there for money. We had managed to keep our lives freeloader-free and I was afraid that was changing.

"I'm not asking for a hand out. It would be a loan. After Michael, well, when it's all over I'll have to sell his company. I've already got someone all lined up. I told Michael we should just go ahead and sell, but he said that until he's dead and gone he's not giving anything up. At any rate, you'd have your money back in less than a year."

I watched Rachel explain how she's already had to think about what she's going to do when her husband dies within the year. It made me want to write her a check for whatever amount she needed. But years of being Luke Weston's daughter and Will Meyer's wife kicked in and I approached the situation with a little more of my head than my heart.

"I'm so sorry you're going through this, Rachel. I don't think it's a good idea to just write you a check. It isn't that I don't want to help. I just need to be, well, careful. I hope you understand," I told her.

"Yes, of course. Thank you anyway." I grabbed Rachel's hand to stop her as she began to stand. I wasn't going to be cold and heartless and not help at all. I just knew that I needed more information than she had provided.

"I think we can help, but that it would be best to send any payments directly to the hospital."

"Oh!" She sat back down, her eyes just a little brighter. "Well, I don't have any of that with me."

"That's okay. I think it's best to give me a few days to consider what we can do to help and then get back together. I'll contact you as soon as I have an answer. Then maybe you can come back by and we'll chat?" I raised my eyebrows and gave her a thin-lipped smile.

Rachel breathed a sigh of relief and I watched her body relax. "Thank you, Layla. You have no idea what this means to us."

"Don't thank me yet," I cautioned. I knew we would help in some way. I just didn't know what that was going to look like quite yet.

As I closed the door behind Rachel that day, my first thought was to talk to Mom. I wanted to do the right thing but I wanted to protect Will, too. It wasn't about the money. I knew Will would want to see Michael, but I had no idea if Michael wanted to see him. Seeing as Rachel was keeping her plea for help a secret from him, I had a feeling Michael's feelings about connecting with Will hadn't changed. More than that, I needed to find out if Rachel's story was true.

Now that I'm sitting here in front of Mom and Eliana, I'm not sure telling them is the best idea. They'll tell me not to keep this from Will but they don't understand. If Michael doesn't want to see Will it will break his heart again. They weren't there when my husband cried himself to sleep because his hopes of having a brother had been crushed. I won't let him get hurt again.

"You know, I can't even remember now," I lie. "It must be New Mommy Brain! But I will tell you this: Tyler and Caroline are together!"

"Oh thank God you know! It's been awful keeping that from you!" Eliana says with relief. She and Mom look at each other and both give a sigh.

"Geez! Everyone knew?" I whine.

"It wasn't our choice to keep it from you," Mom defends. "I wanted to, but Will said Caroline would tell you when she was ready."

"Well, 'ready' happened today when I walked in on the two of them canoodling on her porch!" We laugh and spend the rest of our time together speculating on how long it will be before Tyler proposes. Then we throw out our own ideas for how we'll hijack Caroline's wedding and help Carol with the planning. It's a fun afternoon that reminds me what a lucky girl I am.

I leave the moms and make my way to the mall to do a little shopping. I don't plan on buying a lot since my goal is to have Wes kick me back into shape.

Wes. That's it.

Four pairs of jeans and a couple of tops later I'm back in my car and going straight to Wes' office. Hopefully he's there and not out on the training field.

Wes started his own security company a few years ago. He hired some legit guys but also gave jobs to some of the good guys who used to work for Meyer. A lot of them have steady gigs as personal security for the high-powered, while some of them work contract jobs for celebrities who come to town and need someone who knows the area.

I luck out when I pull in the parking lot and see Wes' car.

"Hey you! Where are my girls?" Wes asks as I knock on the frame of his door.

"Hey! *I'm* great, by the way!" I joke. No one tells you that after you have kids no one is going to care about how you're doing. They only want to see the baby, or in my case, babies. It's not as big a deal as one might think because, honestly, I only care about the babies, too.

"Whatever! Where are my girls?" Wes laughs.

"They're home with Will. I just had lunch with Mom and Eliana," I tell him.

"That's right. El said she was seeing you today. What brings you by?"

"Well," I begin. "I'll start off with my first reason. I need you to throw some Marine training at me and help me get back to my pre-baby size. I want to get fit."

"Sure! You've put me through enough that I'd be happy to kick your ass a little bit!"

"Ha, ha, ha! Very funny!" I punch his arm, one of the pieces of evidence that Wes will know how to get me into shape.

"What's the other reason you're here?" he asks. I bite my lip knowing I'm about to ask Wes to keep something from Eliana and Luke. Wes cocks his head. "Layla?" he says suspiciously.

"I need an address."

Chapter 3

I open our front door to what looks like a group of carolers. It seems that all of our dinner guests decided to show up at the same time. One by one, Mom and Dad, Caroline, Tyler, Caroline's parents, Wes, and Eliana file through the door, offering hugs as they enter.

Caroline is going back to Los Angeles tomorrow, and I made her promise to come to dinner before she deserted us again. Her Decorator-to-the-Stars status is seriously putting a damper on our relationship. It's really hard to get in touch with her when she's gallivanting all over the country!

"You guys get a group rate on a cab or something," Will says walking into the foyer with both girls in his arms. He doesn't usually walk around with both of them, but he knows in less than a minute they'll be snuggled in the arms of any one of our friends or family.

"Can it and give me one of those baby dolls!" Caroline demands. She scoops Natalie up in her arms and squeals. "Oh my goodness! You're so big already!"

"She wouldn't seem so big if you came around more often," I chastise teasingly.

"Don't you listen to your mommy, Natalie," Caroline says in a high, baby-sounding voice as she tickles Natalie's button nose. "After you, your sister, and your daddy, she loves me most."

"Alright, alright! C'mon in everyone. Can Will get anyone a drink while I finish getting dinner ready?" We all shuffle to the back of the house where the kitchen is. We remodeled last year and turned the kitchen seating area to more of a lounge with couches and short tables. Everyone always gathers in the kitchen, so it seemed like a more appropriate design.

Will opens a few bottles of our favorite wine while I take the roast from the oven. I let it rest and finished whipping my homemade mashed potatoes.

"You've outdone yourself again, Layla," Dad tells me as I return from laying the girls down for their nap.

"Thank you!" I smile. "We're so glad everyone could come tonight. I know it was short notice, but *Caroline* didn't tell me she was going to be in town; otherwise, I would have set this up a while ago." I smirk at Caroline and she narrows her eyes at me before we both laugh.

"Well, because I don't want to be accused of keeping information from anyone again, I have a little announcement," Caroline begins.

Oh my goodness! I think. This is it! Tyler has already proposed and she's going to announce it here tonight!

"I'm going to France!"

Not the announcement I was expecting, but still exciting.

"That's awesome! When? How long will you be gone?" I ask. I watch Tyler as he smiles at Caroline, so genuinely happy for her.

"I leave in about two months. We're still finalizing the details. And, well, I'll be gone … indefinitely." Caroline's expression is one of both excitement and trepidation. I see why when I look at the face sitting next to her. The smile on Tyler's face fades. This part of the story must be news to him.

Before I can say anything, one of the babies starts stirring and then lets out a full-blown whale of a cry.

"I'm sorry," I say with a breathy laugh. "Motherhood calls. I'll be right back."

It's not time for their nap to be over, so I tip-toe into the nursery and find that Claire has lost her thumb under her long sleeve. On top of that, she's had an explosive diaper. Natalie, who can sleep through anything, is still gently purring in the other crib. I change Claire's diaper, put her in pajamas with shorter sleeves, and rock her for a few minutes before I lay her back down. Now that she has her thumb and a clean bum, she drifts back to sleep peacefully.

Stepping off the last stair I hear Tyler and Caroline arguing in the front room.

"How could you drop a bomb like that in front of everyone? Why did you keep that from me?" Tyler says in a strong tone just above a whisper.

"I only found out the other day that they want me to work on several projects while I'm there. There's an ambassador and even some celebrities. George Clooney is having his whole Lake Como home remodeled and the firm wants me to lead the redesign!" Caroline counters.

"Clooney's place is in Italy." Silence fills the space after Tyler's observation. I can imagine the blank look on Caroline's face. "Are you kidding me? You're going to Italy, too?"

More silence and I see the edge of Tyler as he paces around the room before finding a place hidden from me.

"I don't know why you're so upset. We already talked and said that we could work the whole long distance thing out." Caroline is trying to explain herself but falling short. I'm her best friend and even I can't back her up on this.

"That was when it was for six months max. Now I'm supposed to just wait until you decide you're done gallivanting all over Europe? I can't believe you would do this to us, Care!"

"I can't just say 'no' to them. This is a huge opportunity for my career, Ty. I need you to understand that."

"All I understand is that you didn't have enough respect for me … for us … to talk to me about this first. You don't think I'm thrilled for you to have this opportunity?" Tyler breathes a heavy sigh. "Of course I am."

"Then what's the problem?" I can't believe Caroline just asked him that.

"The problem is that I would have been willing to have a conversation about it with the woman I thought was just as much in love with me as I am with her. But because you went about it the way that you did, I'm not sure if you're that woman."

Tyler steps into the foyer and is startled by my presence. He opens his mouth to say something, but I think he's at a loss for words. I give him a tight-lipped, sympathetic smile before he walks out the front door.

When Caroline emerges she is wiping the evidence of their emotional conversation from beneath her eyes.

"Hey," I say softly to her.

"Oh, hey. Sorry about that," she says. She takes a cleansing breath and regains her composure. "He'll come around."

"I don't know, Care. It was kind of a crappy thing to do," I tell her honestly. "Why didn't you just tell him before?"

"It's complicated, Layla," she says dismissively.

"It doesn't sound complicated. It sounds like you first told him you would be gone for six months and now you're telling him you don't know when you'll be home."

"So, what? You're married with kids and now you know everything there is to know about relationships?" Caroline crosses her arms in front of her defensively to match her tone.

"Wait. What? Is that what you think *I* think?" I furrow my brow at Caroline's response. "What I'm saying has nothing to do with me being married. It has to do with basic common courtesy."

"Yeah, well, not everyone has the fairytale romance you and Will had, you know."

"First of all, I wouldn't call what Will and I went through a fairytale. Secondly, what is going on? Since when have you and I not been able to be straight with each other?"

Caroline stands there just staring at me. I search her eyes looking for some clue, a hint of something that would tell me what she isn't saying. I've never seen Caroline like this before, and it's kind of freaking me out.

Suddenly I am scared that maybe she is right. Maybe having kids is going to eternally change things between us. Maybe we will never connect in the same way we have for almost ten years now.

Caroline walks to the door and lets her hand linger on the knob for a moment before she speaks. "Can you just tell my parents I walked back to the house?"

Not sure there is anything else I could say, and feeling that perhaps what we all need is some time to breathe, I nod my reply and watch her walk out the door.

"Hey, babe. Did Caroline just leave?" Will asks as he approaches me from behind.

"Yeah."

"Um … what happened between you two?"

"I have no idea."

Mr. and Mrs. Jackson are making apologies to Mom and Dad as they enter the foyer.

"She's very overwhelmed right now," I hear Carol say. "An overwhelmed Caroline does not have the clearest of heads."

"No kidding. She just bit mine off," I say.

"She's got a long flight back to L.A. tomorrow. I'm sure by the time she lands she'll have come to her senses."

Mom closes the door behind the Jacksons and everyone turns their attention to me. I stand there waiting for someone to speak but it appears they're all waiting on me.

"What?"

"Are you alright, dear?" Eliana asks.

"I'm fine. People fight. She'll call me tomorrow and we'll be fine." But Caroline and I have never fought before. Maybe it is a sign that we really are growing apart.

"Yes, I'm sure by tomorrow night you two will have everything worked out," Mom says in her Mom way.

Mom and Eliana offered to help with the dishes but I told them to go home. I find cleaning the kitchen to be very cathartic. It will give me time to think.

"Layla, could we talk for a minute about the ass-kicking training I'm going to give you?" Wes asks. He gives me a look that tells me our conversation is going to have zero to do with my getting back in shape.

"Sure. Babe, do you mind checking on the girls? I put Claire in different pajamas. Can you make sure she's warm enough?" I ask Will as Mom and Dad leave.

"I'm going to the car. Don't be long, darling," Eliana says to Wes. "I'll talk to you soon, Layla." I give her a hug goodbye and watch as she closes the door behind her.

Wes stands in front of me with his hands in his pockets. He pulls one hand out and holds a folded piece of paper in front of me. I reach out to take it but Wes pulls it away before my fingers can grasp it.

"Are you going to tell me now why I'm giving you Michael Meadows' address?" Wes stands there with his serious *give-me-answers* face that no one can deny.

I let out a defeated sigh before I answer. "His wife Rachel came to see me last week. Apparently Michael is really sick and she asked me for financial help. I just need to go see for myself that it's true."

"And Will doesn't know." Wes has a way of making statements out of what other people would ask as questions.

"I'm not telling him anything until I know for sure. He'll be crushed if he gets his hopes up of having a relationship with Michael only to find out it was all a lie."

Wes just nods as he listens to my explanation.

"You're not going to try and talk me out of it?" I question.

"I think we both know that would be an exercise in futility," he says with a smirk. He is right. He knows all too well that once I set my mind to something, there is little to nothing that could make me change my mind.

"So what if it's true?" Wes asks.

"Then we'll help them as much as we can. And we'll hope that Michael will want to make peace with the past and with Will before it's too late," I tell him.

"And what if it's not?"

"If it's not, well ... I have a Wes Furtick for that." I smile. Wes releases the paper to me and I slide it in my back pocket.

"What do you have a Wes Furtick for?" Will asks as he descends the stairs next to us. He's smiling and has huge wet spot on his shoulder revealing the time he spent with a baby in his arms.

"She asked me to whip her into shape," Wes answers. He puts his arm around my shoulder and squeezes me to him. I reciprocate the hug and wrap my arms around his waist.

"Ah," Will responds. "Just don't let her fade away to nothing. I like her post-baby body." Will pulls me from Wes and wraps his own arms around me and kisses the top of my head.

"On *that* note," Wes says. "I'm going. El is waiting in the car." Wes kisses my temple and gives Will a hug before letting himself out.

I'm quiet as Will and I clear the dinner table and tidy the kitchen. On top of this whole thing with Michael, now I have to figure out what's going on with Caroline and what I'm going to do about it. I understand her being overwhelmed. It must be a wonderfully stressful place to be in. She has an incredible opportunity to travel Europe and be the interior designer to a Who's Who list of people. But she also has Tyler, and from the look in her eyes the other day I know that she loves him. How does one get everything they ever wanted and have to choose between them?

"You want to talk about it?" he asks.

I sit on the couch in the lounge and put my feet up on one of the small round tables in front of me. Twisting my head, I stretch my neck and relieve some of the tension that has been building. Reading my body language, Will instinctively brings me a glass of wine as he takes a seat next to me with his own glass.

"You're the best husband ever." I take the glass from him and take a sip of the red elixir. "I'm trying to understand how things got so out of control but I'm at a loss."

"She should have told him, Layla." Will's tone is a little defensive.

"Yes, she should," I reply.

"Really?"

"Yeah." I furrow my brow at Will. "Did you think I was going to side with Caroline?"

"Well, yeah. Isn't there some girl club rule that says you have to support each other no matter what?"

"No," I say with my own defensiveness. "Well, sometimes. But not when she's so obviously wrong. I mean ... was she *trying* to push him away? Why would she drop that kind of bomb on him right in front of everyone?"

"I don't know. I've known Caroline a long time, and I have to say I'm pretty surprised by her behavior. Maybe she's just changed. Maybe we've all changed." Will slips his arm around me and I rest my weary head on his shoulder.

"I don't want us to have all changed."

"We have to change, Layla. No one can stay the same. We have to grow and mature. I can't be the same person I was at seventeen now. I want to be better than that. For you. For the girls. And, like it or not, we've just moved into a different place than all our friends."

"Not all our friends. Chris is married. So is Gwen," I rebut.

"True. And if they lived in town, I'm sure we'd see them more often as married people. But we're parents now and that puts us in a whole new bracket. Our priorities are entirely different than our friends without kids." Will shifts and turns to face me. "Caroline isn't married and has the opportunity of a lifetime. She should take it because she needs to seize the opportunity of a lifetime within the lifetime of the opportunity. One day, going out on this kind of adventure won't even be a consideration because her family will come first."

"I know. And I want her to go. It may or may not be because I want an in to meet George Clooney," I joke. Will looks at me with confused eyes. "Oh, you didn't hear that part. She's actually going to Italy too because the design firm is redoing Clooney's Lake Como place." Will's eyes widen with astonishment. "I know, right?"

"Clooney aside…"

"Yes, Clooney aside." I laugh but the smile quickly fades. "You should have seen the way she was looking at me. It was like ... it was like I didn't know the person standing in front of me."

"I think Carol is right. Just give her some time to come to her senses and things will work out." Will sits back against the couch again and we sit together, sipping wine and enjoying the silence of the house and each other's company. I love our new normal life.

The doorbell rings and we look at each other with puzzled expressions. It's not that late, but no one ever comes by at this time. We walk to the door together and a rush of fear washes over me that it might be Rachel again. When Will opens the door and reveals Tyler standing on the other side, I let out the breath I didn't realize I was holding.

"Hey," he says sheepishly. "Do you mind if I come in?"

Tyler looks beaten down. His eyes are swollen like he's been crying and one of his hands is wrapped in a hand towel. By the blood on it, I'd say he lost a fight with a wall.

"Of course. Come in," Will tells him.

"No offense, Layla, but can I talk to Will alone?" Tyler asks.

"Sure. I'll check on the girls and head to bed. Take your time." I look down at Tyler's injured hand and back at him. "Will can get you some ice for that. And there's some ibuprofen and bandages in the pantry."

"Thanks, Layla."

"It's going to work out," I tell him confidently. "You two could finish cleaning the kitchen while you talk!" I wink and nudge Will before I kiss him goodnight and give Tyler a hug.

I check on the girls and they are still snug like two little bugs. I'm still in awe of them. Still in awe of the path my life has taken. There was a time I couldn't have even begun to dream of loving someone the way I love Will, let alone the way I love Natalie and Claire. And I never dreamed I would be loved the way I am loved by Will and Mom and Dad. There isn't anything I wouldn't do to protect that love.

I take the address Wes gave me out of my pocket and stare at it as I consider the best time for me to go. I'll have to do it soon since Will is on his way back to into the office full time. Michael and his wife live in Cleveland, North Carolina. I've never heard of it and have no clue how far it is, but a Google search will fix that.

The only thing left is to find out if Rachel's story is true, or if she's going to be sorry she ever stepped foot in my house.

Chapter 4

It's been a week since Wes gave me Michael's address. Will is going back to work in a few days so this might be my last chance to go before I have to get one of our mothers to come and watch the girls. They'll want to know where I'm going, which isn't a problem except that if I tell them I'm going shopping, they'll pull out the double stroller and want to come with me. Telling Will I'm going shopping leads only to him being more than willing to stay home with the girls.

I trot down the stairs having searched for driving directions to the mysterious Cleveland, North Carolina. It should take me less than an hour, so if I leave in the next thirty minutes I can be there and back before lunch.

"Okay! The girls have been fed and are enjoying their morning nap," I shout as I make my way to the kitchen. As I turn the corner into the room, Will is putting his jacket on and zipping up his laptop case.

"Hey. Uh … where are you going?" I ask him.

"I've got to run into the office for a bit, and then check on some things in manufacturing." Noticing that I am fully dressed, shoes and all, he asks, "Were you going somewhere?"

My shoulders slump and I twist my mouth to the side. "I *was*."

"I'll be back before four. Can you go then?"

"No. I can't," I begin. "I mean … I didn't find the things I was looking for when I went shopping last time. With you going back to work in a few days I know this is my last real chance to go. After that I'm going to have to take the girls and one of our moms with me. I guess I'm just looking for some final 'me' time. Does that sound selfish?"

Will stands next to me as I sit in one of the bar stools at the counter. I lean into him as he wraps his arms around me.

"I can stay home."

"Really?" I say, perking up. "I should be home before lunch!"

Will laughs at my enthusiasm and brushes the hair that has fallen in my face.

"Go. Have fun. Buy something sexy."

"Well, you did just rearrange your day for me. I think that my husband is deserving of something sexy later." I reach up and pull Will's face to mine and kiss him. The kiss quickly becomes passionate and Will is pulling my shirt out from being tucked into my jeans.

"I said sexy *later*," I muster when Will moves from my lips to my neck. "If you don't let me go now, I'm not going to have time to find something sexy!"

Will gives one last kiss to my neck and breathes a heavy sigh before emerging from the covering of my hair. "Fine!"

I grab is face again and kiss him hard.

"You are not a fair woman. You need to leave now, or I'm going to be forced to have my way with you!"

"Okay! Okay! I'll be back soon! I love you!" I snatch my purse from its place hanging on the end of the staircase railing and close the door behind me.

I've run through in my head all the scenarios I can think of and what I would say. If I get out there and it all turns out to be a lie, I'll simply reflect on how Will handled Marlene and Holly and then fill Michael and Rachel in on their fate if they choose to continue their charade.

If Rachel can show me those medical bills, and if it's clear that Michael has less than a year to live, then we'll do the right thing and help them. I'd stipulate that Michael has to be willing to make amends with Will, but I'm not sure I can do that. It's not like I'm going to refuse to help them.

I make a stop at the outlet mall and pick up a few tops I held off on buying last time, along with that something sexy and a pair of heels that catch my eye as I walk by. I'll need something to show Will when I get home. I don't like being sneaky like this, but I will be sneaky every day of the week and twice on Sunday if it protects my husband from heartache.

The drive to the Meadows' is beautiful. There isn't a lot out this way, making for a very peaceful time with my thoughts. I can't help but think of Caroline and wonder what is going on with her. I've never seen her act the way she did that night. She was completely selfish and unreasonable. And the way she snapped at me? I hate to think that Will might be right about this. Maybe she's changed. We're not kids anymore, and she's been in Los Angeles and New York for years now. I suppose there's just a different way of life in those cities. But why get into a relationship with Tyler, of all people, if she didn't think it was going to have long-term potential? There's something going on here, and I'm going to have to get to the bottom of it. At least my friends can rest assured that there's one area I haven't changed a bit in.

I follow the instructions of my Hugh Jackman-sounding GPS and turn onto a road that quickly ditches the asphalt for dirt. As my Hugh tells me that my destination is ahead, I'm left squeezing my eyebrows together in confusion. There's not much ahead of me but land, and lots of it. It's not until I pass a huge cluster of thick and brushy trees that I see the house. It's an older farmhouse with a carport instead of a garage, and the front porch is one tiny step up and covers the length of the house.

I approach the path to the front door and a large dog appears from the side of the house where there is a massive clearing. He's galloping toward me and I can feel my nerves racing. I quicken my pace but don't run, as I don't want to encourage him to come at me any faster. In a matter of seconds, his pace slows and he comes to a grinding halt. He surveys the land and me and then lays himself down for a rest.

"That's Bob," Rachel says from the front door. I turn my attention to her and take a relieved breath. She doesn't seem very excited to see me. I could be showing up here with a blank check for all she knows, yet she's guarded. "His size is deceiving. He doesn't have a vicious bone in his body."

"I can see that," I say with a nervous laugh. I don't know why I'm so nervous. I'm the one holding the cards here.

"If I had known you were coming today …" she begins.

"Oh, well, you know … I just thought I'd pop by."

She steels herself and opens the screen door. "Won't you come in?"

I smile and walk the remaining length of the path to the porch and inside. The house is filled with a mix of modern and antique items. There's a turn-of-the-century grandfather clock positioned next to a couch I'm certain I saw in a Haverty's catalog a year or so ago, and a vintage baby grand piano in the front window. The only places with any continuity are the walls. They are filled with old pictures of what I assume were the original inhabitants of the home. Many of the photos are brown and all of the frames look aged.

"Your home is lovely," I say.

"It was my mama's. Well, it was my great grand-daddy's first. My grandfather was born in this house. The room right at the top of the stairs." Rachel pauses, grabbing hold of the wooden globe finial on the bannister. "Would you like a tour?"

"Maybe another time. I thought we could talk some more about your situation," I reply.

"Right. Of course." Rachel leads me through the dining room and kitchen to a back sunroom. There is a large, round table and five director's chairs situated around it. Potted plants sporadically line the room, accentuating the beautiful view.

Rachel excuses herself and returns shortly with two glasses of lemonade, setting them on the table in front of us.

"So, Rachel, what is it that you and Michael do? I mean, you said he had his own business." I take a sip of the lemonade and it tastes just about as fresh as it comes.

"We own a hot air balloon company." It takes a moment for that to register with me. I've never thought of it, but, yeah, I guess someone has to own and operate a hot air balloon company. There have to be hundreds of them around the country. "I get that look a lot."

"I'm sorry. I suppose it took me a second to digest that. I've never met anyone who owned a hot air balloon company. I've actually never met anyone who's ever been in a hot air balloon before.

"It's pretty amazing, actually. Michael is a certified balloon pilot."

"How did he get into that? I know it was some years ago, but I thought Michael was in advertising."

"It's a funny story, really," she begins. "It was my family's business. Michael brought his girlfriend up here to propose to her. We did a lot of those. Well, he got her out to the clearing where the balloon was all ready to go, but when he took her blindfold off she freaked out. She started yelling at him that if he really knew her he would have known how terrified of heights she was and would have never brought her out here."

"Oh my gosh!" I laugh. "That's terrible!"

"It got worse. Apparently they drove up in her car, so she grabbed the keys and left him here!"

Now we're both laughing and it feels like two sisters-in-law just sitting around, shooting the breeze. It fills me with conflicted feelings of not wanting Michael to be sick, but wanting Rachel's story to be true so that we can begin to build a relationship with them.

"So what happened?"

"Well, my dad gave him a refund because he felt so badly for him, and then I drove him back to Charlotte. The rest is history."

"That's a really great story, Rachel," I say.

"It made for interesting conversations when he came up here to see me. But it opened the door for my dad to be the father Michael never had. So when my dad asked Michael if he'd take over the company, it was a no-brainer. It became Michael's family business, too." Rachel looks out into the open field from where she indicated the balloons take off. I can see it pains her to think about selling their family business.

"Rachel, why don't you just take over the business? Why do you have to sell it?" I wondered.

"You have to be a certified pilot. I just run the books. I've never made time to get all my flight hours in, and now it's too late. Between trying to run the company as long as Michael is able and taking him to doctor's appointments in Charlotte, there's no way I could do it now." Rachel takes a deep breath and looks at me purposefully. "Look, Layla, I want to apologize for just showing up the way I did. I wasn't right for me to come ask you for money like that. I'm very sorry."

"You don't need to apologize," I begin.

"Yes, I do. And I want you to know that we don't need anything from you. The buyer for the company agreed to pay what we were asking … and I found a buyer for the house and the land. Between all of that, we should be good."

If I thought she was in pain before, I was wrong. This girl's whole world is about to disintegrate. Not only is she going to lose her husband, but now she's going to lose her family business and the family property.

Whoa! Hold on there, Layla, I tell myself. *You still haven't determined if Rachel's story is true or not.*

"Well, why don't we take a look at how Will and I might be able to help anyway? We'd like to if we can."

She darts her eyes as if searching for something inside her head.

"It's, um." Rachel searches for the right words. I don't know what to say to her now. Had she said she was still interested in my help, I would have asked her for the medical bills. Now that she's recanted her request I have nothing.

I suppose I should be fine with her deciding to do whatever it takes to cover these expenses on her own. Something about it isn't sitting well with me, though. I know I showed up here unexpectedly, but she's been extremely uncomfortable almost the entire time. How does she go from things being desperate enough to show up on my doorstep to ask for financial help, to all of the sudden getting asking price for the company and finding a buyer for their property?

"Rachel … are you being straight with me about Michael?"

"What? You think I made up …" she stands in feigned disgust. No, she bolts up out of her chair in telenovela fashion, dramatic and with an audible gasp. "I think you need to leave now."

I stand and follow her to the door she is already half way to. I feel like a switch got flipped and I'm now in the presence of someone entirely different.

"I didn't mean to offend you. Please understand … we've had our share of people wanting something from the Meyer name. It wasn't personal. We just have to be … safe." This is my apology that isn't really an apology because I don't make apologies for protecting my family.

"I'm sure." Rachel stands with the screen door open, her body propping it in place.

With a polite nod I pass her and step off the porch, not looking back until I'm in my car that is already facing the house. I watch the door close and the screen door bounce closed after it. Surveying the house, I catch movement from an upstairs window. Michael has pulled the curtain to the side and is watching me leave. We make eye contact just long enough for me to know exactly how he feels about me showing up at his home today. I'm not the one he should take issue with. Had his wife not come to me first, I would never have trekked out here in an effort to verify her story.

He darts away from the window and doesn't return in the few seconds I linger before putting the car in reverse and making my way back down the long dirt road. Still unsure if Rachel's story is true, I imagine one of two things is happening in their living room right now: Michael is either giving Rachel a tongue lashing for having made me aware of their very personal situation or for letting me drive away without writing a check.

Once I'm back on the highway and know where I'm going to get home, I call Wes on the car's Bluetooth speaker.

"Hey, Layla. Ready for that ass kicking?" Wes' laugh echoes through the car.

"Yes, but that's not why I'm calling. I need you to do something else for me … please?"

"What are you getting yourself into?" he says, his jovial tone now gone.

"I just paid a visit to the Meadows' home. Rachel was totally uneasy the whole time I was there. It was weird," I tell him.

"Of course it was weird. You showed up unannounced to their home, Layla. What were you expecting?" There's a chastisement in Wes' tone. He likes to get fatherly with me sometimes. I don't disparage him for it. I just need him to hear where I'm coming from.

"I expected her to get excited because she thought I was there to tell her we were going to help them. I did *not* expect her to take back her request and tell me that she had decided to sell the family's century-old property! Who does that? I mean, who does that before they know if the person they've asked for help is going to help or not?" I take a breath and steady myself. I'm getting worked up and I really don't need to. What I need is more information. "Listen, I'm telling you, it just didn't sit right with me. I have a feeling she was telling me the truth about their situation. If that's the case, I want to help them. I was hoping she'd clear it up today and that I wouldn't have to ask you for anymore help, but …"

"But you want me to check all the avenues to see if we can corroborate Rachel's story," he says, completing my sentence.

"Yeah."

"And at what point are you going to tell Will about all this?" he asks.

"When I know as many of the facts as possible. If she's lying, then we can nip it in the bud before it goes any further. If it's all true, well, I know Will won't just sit by."

"Even if Michael still isn't interested in making peace?"

I'm silent a good twenty seconds before I respond. This is the hardest part. I can't stand the thought of Will be devastated yet again at Michael's rejection. But it's not in our nature to let someone go through something so terrible without helping. Will always says that being generous never came back to bite anyone in the ass. So we'll be generous.

"Even if Michael still isn't interested in making peace."

I pull up to the house and stretch my neck on either side. I don't like deceiving Will about where I went today, but until I have more answers I can't tell him. When it all comes out, I'll explain to him my reasons for not having been forthcoming with him. Once he knows, he'll understand. I'm sure of it.

I open the door slowly because there is a good chance the babies are still sleeping. They've been alternating days with a two-hour nap one day and then a three-hour nap the next. With the craziness of the day, I can't seem to remember if yesterday was two or three hours.

Stepping into the foyer, I hear the giggles of my two little munchkins and the laughter of the man who practically worships their chubby little feet. Will is making weird noises that the girls find to be the funniest thing they have ever heard. It is spectacular to witness.

"Well hello there!" I say cheerily as I enter the kitchen lounge. The girls are sitting in their Bumbos and Will is lying on his belly in front of them. He gives Claire zerberts on her tiny feet. When she laughs, Natalie laughs and I swear points at her.

"Hi, Mommy! Should Mommy get zerberts next?" Will asks the girls. They are still giggling and I almost give Will permission just so I can watch them laugh again.

"Uh, no!" I laugh. "How was your day? I got to thinking that it was good for you to have this time with them, seeing as you're going back to work full time." I come sit on the floor next to Will and tickle Natalie's toes. She giggles and a smile covers my entire face.

"It was great. They slept about two and a half hours and I got some work done. Then they ate. They like that cereal stuff," he tells me.

"Oh good!" I say. "Do you ever stop to think about the conversations we have now? Poopy diapers and naps and feedings and zerberts. Gone are the days of sitting at the edge of the dock talking, laughing, and you giving me music lessons. No more picnics on the dock either. Our lives have changed so much."

Will sits up and examines my face.

"Does this have a little more to do with Caroline than us?" he asks.

He takes my hand in his, threading our fingers together.

"I don't know. Maybe. It certainly isn't a negative commentary on our life. I love our life! We fought way too hard for this life not to love it!" I give a small laugh. The kind you can give only when something is so far in your past that you chuckle because you know that experience made you the victorious survivor that you are today. "But this thing with Caroline … I just can't believe that she's changed, not this drastically at least. You should have seen the way they looked at each other. There's no way she just doesn't give a rip about how Tyler feels. I just wish I could sit down and talk with her."

"You want to go see her, don't you?" Will smiles, knowing the answer.

I twist my mouth into a smile. "I do."

"Well, find out from Carol when she's going to be in New York and go," he suggests.

"What about you and the girls? I've never been away from them for more than a few hours." Even the thought of leaving them makes my stomach churn.

"It'll only be a couple of days. I'll be with them, and Mom and Claire will come over to make sure I don't break them," he chuckles. "We've already been talking about an anniversary trip in a few months. And we promised ourselves that we weren't going to be *those* parents who get so wrapped up in our kids that we forget who we were before they arrived. Remember what Nana Grace said? 'One day your children will grow up and move out. Decide now who you want to be when that happens: roommates or lovers?'"

It was a great piece of advice.

I smile at Will. "Lovers. Definitely lovers."

Will kisses me, and the girls start to giggle again, which makes us giggle, too. The sound of their laughter makes me so grateful for the changes. All of the changes.

I used to think that once I got to the other side of reclaiming myself with my move to Davidson all those years ago, I'd be set for life. What I'm realizing is that all the changes that I've been through are evidence of growth. No one wants their life to be stagnant, so I'm going to enjoy this ride. I'm going to hold onto my husband and my baby girls and travel this winding and sometimes bumpy road with them. And I'm going to try not to blink too much so I don't miss a single second of it.

Chapter 5

Of course on a night when Will and I want to get romantic the twins would give us a hard time about going to bed. It takes us an hour to get them to settle down. I'm worried though, since their diapers seem to be telling us something isn't quite right in their tummies. Funny that the wrong colored poop now causes me to be filled with concern.

"They're fine," Will reassures me as he leads me from the nursery. I've been watching them sleep for twenty minutes just to make sure they are okay.

I take a seat in the kitchen lounge as instructed by my husband and wait for him to return with a glass of wine.

"Are you really that worried?" he asks.

I take the glass from him and take a sip. "Yes and no. I know they're going to be fine. Dr. Anderson said they'd be adjusting to the rice cereal so I expected something." I tilt my head from side to side, stretching out the tension that is building in my neck. "I'm trying, but it's hard to unwind when I'm so focused on the girls."

Will puts his wine glass on the table in front of us. "Well maybe I can help with that."

He shifts in his seat and nudges me to move as well so I'm sitting with my back to him. Gently he begins massaging my neck and shoulders. It doesn't take long before I realize I should put my wine glass down before I become so relaxed that it slips from my hand.

I lower my chin and Will moves his hand up the nape of my neck and into my hair and then back down to my neck and shoulders.

"I don't know what it is, but your touch seems to be a cure-all," I moan.

"If you think this is good, let me lay this move on you."

Will moves my hair to one side and begins kissing my neck and that special spot behind my ear. It feels amazing and I instantly want more. I turn around and push Will against the back of the couch, throwing one leg over and straddling him. I take his face in my hands and crush my lips against his. His hands have my backside in a firm grip, pulling my body closer to him. I unbutton his shirt and run my hands over his hot, smooth skin. My hands have a few seconds of longing when Will lifts my shirt off and tosses it on the floor.

"You sure know how to make a girl relaxed," I breathe in between assaulting Will's neck with hungry kisses.

"Good to know my work is appreciated," he says in a low voice.

"Oh, I'm about to show you just how appreciated it is."

I stand up and reach behind my back to unclasp my bra when our doorbell rings and everything comes to a screeching halt.

"You have *got* to be kidding me! Are you expecting someone?" I ask with a deep sigh.

"No. And quite frankly, they can stay out there." Will grabs a belt loop on my jeans and pulls me back to him. "Let your husband take care of this." He smirks and then kisses me as he reaches behind me to finish what I started.

I was happy to let whoever was at our door to give up and leave, but when they ring the bell again and then knock, I know the night is over. We have to answer the door before they become even more aggressive and wake up the girls.

"I'll go deal with this." Will stands disappointedly and goes to answer the door while I put my shirt back on. All I can think is that whoever it is at the door better have a damn good reason for interrupting us.

I slide my shirt over my head and am halfway to the front door when I hear Will's surprised voice.

"Michael? What … what are you doing here?"

I gasp.

"Ask your wife!" Michael says with a growl just as I enter the foyer. He looks thinner than he should be, and pale. And he's bald. "Who the hell do you think you are, showing up at my home like that?"

"Whoa! I can see you're upset, but you need to back off on how you're speaking to my wife," Will warns. "Why don't we just calm down and have a conversation here?"

Michael stands there, fuming. I don't understand why he's so angry with me. It wasn't like I decided to just show up at his home unannounced for no reason.

"Layla? What is he talking about?"

I'm saved by another knock at the door. Will looks at me and I shrug, just as clueless as he is about who our next unexpected visitor could be.

I open the door and am both nervous and relieved to find Wes standing there. I step aside and let him in without a word.

"Now's not a really good time, Wes," Will says.

"Actually, it appears that now is a perfect time." Wes surveys Michael and hands me a folder with everything I asked him to find. Documentation from Michael's oncologist confirming his diagnosis of pancreatic cancer, the financials for the family business and loan application from the person Rachel said was going to buy it, and the certification of value on Rachel's family land. Everything was there and in order proving that Rachel's story was true. It was all I needed to assure Will that we would be doing the right thing in helping them.

"Will someone please tell me what's going on?" Will cocks his head and looks at me. By *someone* he means me.

I shoot out a heavy breath. "I'm sorry that I showed up unannounced today."

"Today?" Will is shocked and confused.

"Yes. Today," I reiterate. That is going to be another conversation for later: my lying to my husband. "I wouldn't have come had Rachel not come to see me in the first place."

"I've already dealt with her on that. I just came here to tell you that we don't need your charity. Rachel, well, she knows how I feel about the Meyers and wouldn't have crossed that line if she hadn't been feeling desperate." Michael's tone is strong and angry. Even though he just came in from the chilled air, he has beads of sweat framing his forehead and lip.

"Michael, please. You're family, and family—" I begin but Michael is swift to cut me off.

"We are NOT family!" he shouts. He takes a stumbled step to the side as he points his finger at me. Wes moves quickly to his side and helps him to a chair. "Get off me!" he growls as he sits. Wes does as he's ordered but it's clear that Michael is not well. "I'm fine!"

"I'm going to need you to stop shouting. I have two babies asleep upstairs, and if you wake them up we're going to have an even bigger problem than we do right now." Will crosses his arms in front of him commandingly. "So I'm gathering that your wife came to see my wife to ask for help. You referred to 'charity' so I'm going to assume she asked for money."

"I never even suggested she reach out to you," Michael says, a little more calm now.

"She told me you'd be upset if you knew she came to see me," I tell him. I want him to know just how desperate she was.

"So now I know why Michael is here. What's your involvement in this, Wes?"

"I'm going to let your wife answer that since she promised to tell you what was going on," Wes answers. I narrow my eyes at him for throwing me under the bus at this moment.

"I asked Wes to look into Rachel's story to make sure it was true," I said after a moment.

"You thought my wife would lie about something like this?" Michael protests.

"Something like what?" Will asks for clarification.

Michael and I stare at each other, him daring me to stay silent, me daring him to be forthcoming. I finally unlock my eyes from his and shift them to Wes, who gives me a slight shoulder lift and cock of his head as if to say, "Go ahead. It can't get any worse."

"Michael has pancreatic cancer." I look at Will and wait for his reply. It's hit him like a Mack truck. I wonder if when Michael walked through our door, Will's hopes for a brother boiled to the top. Hearing that Michael is terminally ill changes things.

"I imagine that brings a lot of medical bills, even with insurance," Will muses.

Michael's pride forces his words. "It's nothing we can't handle." He closes his eyes and furrows his brow while he puts his hand on his stomach. It is easy to see that he isn't feeling well.

It takes a minute before Will responds. "Michael, you may not like the Meyer name, and quite frankly, I don't blame you. But my father … our father … isn't here anymore. Layla and I are building a new legacy to the Meyer name. One that comes from a place of wanting to be people who care about others. So, I don't see any reason why we can't help. We'd really be happy and honored to."

I slide my arm around Will's waist, proud that the man I married isn't letting anything keep him from helping someone in need … even their own rejection of said help.

"I said I. DON'T. WANT. YOUR. HELP!" Michael darts up from his seat and takes another stumble to his side. Wes catches him again, only this time Michael doesn't regain his footing or argue. In fact, he doesn't say anything as his body goes limp in Wes' arms.

"Oh my God!" I cry. I run into the kitchen and grab my phone, dialing 911 as fast as I can. Wes and Will confirm that Michael is still breathing, and within minutes an ambulance is pulling into our driveway. Just moments later Mom, Dad, and Eliana are running into the house.

"Oh, thank God!" Mom weeps as she throws her arms around me.

"What are you doing here?" I ask.

"Wes called Eliana and said that we all needed to come. When we heard and then saw the ambulance, I thought the worst," she explains.

"Someone is going to need to stay with the girls." Wes knew that I would insist on going to the hospital and thought ahead. I mouth the words 'thank you' to Wes and run upstairs to check on the girls and grab a coat and a pair of shoes. Within five minutes Will and I are on the highway to the hospital with Wes close behind in his car. It is a silent ride for most of the time.

"Layla, what's going on?" Will's tone is disappointed. "Why didn't you just tell me Rachel came to see you? Why all the lying and sneaking around?"

"I had to know if Rachel was telling the truth. I knew we would help them if she was," I explain.

"You can't just think about what you want to do anymore. We have Natalie and Claire to think about now."

"I understand that, Will. I'm always thinking of them. And part of me thinking of them is thinking of you."

"You're going to have to explain that to me," Will says sternly. He hasn't even heard what I have to say or begun to understand, and he's already put up a wall.

I sigh. "You didn't see what I saw the night Michael walked away from us. My strong and seemingly unbreakable husband lay in my arms and cried an ocean's worth of tears. The hope he had of having a brother was crushed not once, but twice. Marcus was one thing, but for Michael to stand in front of you and reject even the idea of being brothers was worse." Remembering that night brings tears to my eyes. It was the most awful thing I'd ever seen. "I watched you weep out all of those hurt and broken feelings. I had to know that this wasn't just a ploy to get money from us and that they were really in need. If they really needed our help, then we could approach you and Michael having some kind of relationship before it was too late. If it was all a lie, well … I just couldn't watch you get your hopes up only to have them crushed again."

Will reaches across the console and takes my hand. He lifts it to his lips and kisses my knuckles. "I don't like the lying, but I understand. I don't know how, but sometimes I forget just how strong you are. I'm lucky to have you. And … I'm sorry."

"Why are you sorry?" I ask, my eyebrows knitting together..

"I'm sorry you had to see me like that on that night."

I turn in my seat so I can sort of face him. "Don't you ever be sorry about any emotion you have. You once told me that I could laugh, cry, scream at the top of my lungs, or be silent with you anytime I needed. I'm here to catch your tears, too, you know."

Will nods with a smile and I spend the rest of the drive to the hospital explaining the details I have about Michael and Rachel's situation. Apparently Michael was diagnosed with stage-three pancreatic cancer about eight months ago. Surgery wasn't an option, so Michael tried both radiation and chemotherapy. Neither have worked and now they're just biding their time. They have insurance but the deductible is so high that it almost doesn't matter. Even if they are able to pay it, the percentage the insurance company covers is laughable.

I tell Will about their hot air balloon business and Rachel's family's hundred-year-old property. I explain that they've got a buyer for the business and that Rachel is going to sell the family house and land, too, in order to cover the medical bills.

"That's crazy," Will exclaims.

"That's what I thought, too. Rachel said that's what they wanted, but I think it's more what Michael wants," I say.

"Well, I'll just have our account wire the money into their accounts," he says matter-of-factly.

"You can't do that, Will."

"Why not? They need the money or Rachel is going to be destitute after Michael dies." Will's face is scrunched in confusion. For him it seems like an easy solution, which it is. But we still can't do it.

"Because you can't ride up on your white horse with a bushel of money to throw at them. You father threw money around and thought everyone needed to just be grateful for it. People have a choice, a free will. If this is what they want to do, then we have to let them do it."

Will thinks for a few minutes before he speaks. I study him in the silence and in the dim light of the moon and passing headlights. He is distressed. I know Will's heart is full of goodness. It pains him to not be allowed to help someone in need. That was kind of the whole point in keeping the money left to him by his father. He didn't want it at first, but when he realized the good he could do with it the game changed. That's why when they found the bag of money I kicked into Lake Norman, Will let the Town of Davidson use it for refurbishing the Nature Preserve.

Since we got married, we've helped fund local and global organizations that are working to change lives. Our greatest joy comes from giving. That's what makes this so difficult for Will.

"Well, maybe we can change their minds. I'm not going to force them, but I am going to strongly suggest they accept our help. I can't just walk away."

"I know. And that's why I love you."

Chapter 6

The last time I was in this hospital I left with two amazing gifts. Today, though, there are no balloons or flowers in sight, which is typical for the ER waiting room.

Will lets the receptionist know that we are there for Michael Meadows and we settle in for an undetermined amount of time. Wes arrives a few moments after us, finishing a call on his cell.

"So?" he asks, taking a seat across from us.

"They'll let us know when there's something to tell," Will replies.

"I called Rachel. I didn't think she should wait until they treated him to know he was here. It'll take her a while to get here, too, so I figured the sooner she knew, the better," Wes tells us.

"Thank you. I'm sure she appreciated it," I say.

"At first she was a little skeptical. I had to explain to her that Michael had come to see you, which she didn't know."

"Geez! Doesn't anybody tell their spouse where they are anymore?" Will laughs.

"Says the man who dropped off the face of the earth and faked his death." I raise my eyebrows at him.

"Point taken."

"Anyway … she's on her way now." Wes pulls out his phone and sends a few texts to let his staff know he'll probably be late tomorrow.

Mom and Eliana take turns texting Will and me with questions and updates on our sleeping children. I text Mom back and thank her and Eliana for stepping in so quickly, and apologize for not knowing when we'll be home. That is, of course, not an issue for them. They're very good grandmothers.

We sit there for another forty-five minutes before Rachel arrives. In that time we hear absolutely nothing from anyone.

"I'm so sorry," I say to her. "I wish I had something to tell you."

"It's okay." Rachel sits down and her burdens seem to ease off of her shoulders. I watch her face as she looks at us and it occurs to me that maybe she hasn't had anyone by her side during these last eight months.

"Rachel," I begin gingerly. "Is there anyone you'd like us to call for you? Maybe a few friends of yours and Michael's?" I have a feeling I know what she's going to say, but I don't want to put the words in her mouth.

"No. There's no one. We don't really have good friends. Anyone we told about the cancer got scared off once Michael started showing how sick he was. It's amazing how busy people suddenly become. It didn't take long for Michael to decide we weren't telling anyone else." She looks down with lonely eyes. I can't believe Michael has confined her to this prison. He's dying of cancer and she hasn't been allowed to tell anyone?

Oh. It occurs to me that Michael is angry that Rachel broke through their cone of secrecy, but angrier that when she did it, she came to the *Meyers.* It's no wonder he's so angry. We *have* to get him to reconcile with Will.

"Michael Meadows?" The nurse calls his name from the door in search for his family. Rachel stands up and bolts to her. Their voices are low, so their conversation is nothing but a melody of hums and whispers from where we are sitting.

"She said he's stable but that he's suffering from orthostatic hypotension. He's basically really dehydrated, and I'm guessing he got pretty worked up tonight." Will gives her a small nod to confirm her suspicions. "They're moving him to a room on the oncology floor so they can get some fluids in him and monitor him at least overnight. The nurse said to give them about thirty minutes before he's ready to see anyone."

"That's good news," I say softly.

"Well, um," Will begins. He's fighting the urge to say something about helping them financially, but I can see the wheels in his head considering what I said earlier in the car. "Please don't hesitate to contact us. We're here to help in any way we can." He gives her a final nod and we begin to move toward the door.

"Don't leave." Her words are quick and distressed. She is standing there begging us not to leave her in the loneliness she has been living. "Michael may not like it, but we need you. And I'm not talking about the money. I don't even care about that. I just … I can't do this by myself anymore, and you're the only people who seem to care. You could have just let the ambulance bring him here, but you came, too. And then you stayed." She wipes a tear that hadn't yet rolled down her face quite yet and takes a breath. "You're all I have."

I look at Will who is trying to hold back the emotions being stirred up by Rachel's request. While what she's said is beautiful, I just hope Will understands that she's not speaking for Michael. She's speaking for herself, of her own need for family during this time. The hope, though, is that she will be able to express this same passion to Michael as she has to us.

"Of course we'll stay," Will tells her. "Wes, do you think Eliana will mind staying overnight? You're all welcome to, since I don't know when we'll be home."

"Are you kidding? She's probably already set herself up in one of the guest rooms." Wes smiles and pats Will on the shoulder.

"Thank you, Mr. Furtick," Rachel says to him. "I appreciate you calling me when you did." I chuckle to myself at her calling him *Mr.* Furtick. It makes him sound so much more official.

When we get to Michael's room, his nurse is pressing some buttons on a machine that looks to be attached to him. It beeps several times and then flashes a green light that eventually stays solid just as she leaves.

At first Michael only sees Rachel. I know this because his eyes open wider and he smiles at her the way Will smiles at me. It's easy to see how much he loves her. If he only knew how hurt and alone she felt.

"Hi, honey," he says just before his smile fades. "What are they doing here?"

"They came to make sure you were alright … to make sure *I* was alright," she tells him. Michael looks at her and then looks at us. He shifts in the bed, steadying himself before he speaks again.

"Thank you," he says from behind gritted teeth. "I appreciate you staying with Rachel but, as I've been trying to make abundantly clear, we don't need anything from you. Leave."

"No." Rachel's voice is strong and determined.

"Rachel, I told you how I felt about them."

"And now I'm going to tell you how I feel about them." She lifts her chin confidently, knowing that Michael is a captive audience in his hospital bed. "Quite frankly, none of us knows each other at all. But even though they don't know us, and both of us barged in on them—me begging so rudely for money to help us out of the hole, and you causing a scene big enough to put you in the hospital— they're here. They didn't just watch the ambulance drive away with you in it. And they didn't wait for the hospital to call me. They came here to support us. They called me before the hospital would so that I could get here sooner." She takes Michael's hand in hers and soothes her tone. "Now, I know what you've said about Gregory Meyer. But I also know that we've never known a sour thing to be said about Will or Layla. And after what they did tonight, don't you think you owe it to them to stop being such a hard ass?"

The nurse from earlier comes to the door, interrupting the awkward silence that now fills the spaces between us. "Mrs. Meadows? Can I borrow you for a minute? I just have a few things for you to sign."

"Of course," she answers. She raises an eyebrow at her husband as if to tell him to play nicely. Then she gives us a nod as she leaves the room. The silence continues for a moment, no one sure who should speak first.

"I'm trying to figure out what I did to make you dislike me so much," Will says. He's gripping my hand tightly and I think it's because he's trying not to cry. When Michael turns his head and doesn't answer, Will releases my hand and takes a few steps closer, landing at the foot of Michael's bed. "If this is about our father …"

"That man was not my father!" Michael shouts as he snaps his head back to Will.

Will is taken aback, but recovers quickly because he fully understands Michael's sentiment. "I get it. He wasn't really my father either."

"Oh, please! Don't give me that. He didn't put you or your mother out on the street. He stayed, raising you your whole life, which is why I don't trust you. You stayed a bit too close to that tree for my comfort." Michael's face is hard, his nostrils flaring with anger.

There really must be something about how a boy sees his father. Will's half-sisters were much quicker to separate Will from his father. Maybe it was because the parent they identified with taught them how to be strong, independent women. Michael and Marcus never had a real father to teach them what it meant to be a real man. Will had to consciously push through and make the choice every day that he didn't want to be like Gregory Meyer.

"Just because he was there doesn't mean he was a father. I'd rather have had no father than to have had him," Will counters sternly. He softens his tone. "Is that what you're worried about? You think I'm going to be like him?"

Michael chews the inside of his cheek for a moment, contorting his mouth in contemplation.

"It all happened so fast. Finding out about you and the others, and then learning about this man that had hurt my mother so badly. A man that was technically my father. The more I heard about what he had done to so many people, the more concerned I was that I was genetically destined to be like him. And then I thought, what would you be like, the guy who was actually raised by that monster? I just couldn't risk that."

"Well, you found out that *you* are *nothing* like him," I said.

"It would kill me to hurt Rachel the way he hurt my mother. The way he hurt your mother." Michael looks at Will, his eyes beginning to soften.

"And I can testify that Will is nothing like his father at all. He never has been."

"I had the same worries that you did. I didn't know if somewhere down the line I was going to find out I was genetically predisposed to being a douchebag," Will chuckles. "We make our own destiny, Michael. We decide what kind of men we want to be. It looks like character and integrity won out for both of us."

"I don't know …" Michael muses. He looks past us and into the hall where Rachel is standing with the nurse. She has a folder open in front of Rachel and is pointing at several things with a pen. Rachel leans her elbow on the high counter and puts her head in her hand, alternating disbelieving shakes of her head with nods of understanding.

"I think it's worth starting fresh before it's too late. It's at least worth doing for her." Will and Michael lock eyes and I see the first signs of understanding each other. They both love their wives so much that they would do anything for them.

Rachel returns with a stack of papers in her hand. She's tried to freshen herself up, but the redness of her eyes and the apples of her cheeks reveal that she has most definitely been crying. I don't know if the nurse was discussing Michael's prognosis or their outstanding balance. Either way, her state makes me want to beg Michael to let us help them. It doesn't seem fair to Rachel to leave her with nothing when he's gone. She'll have no family business or family home. No place to exist and remember the wonderful life she shared with Michael. Sure, she'll take the pictures of them and hang them in a new space of some little apartment she'll occupy on her own, but it won't be the same. Michael will have never been there. She will never wake up in a bed there and remember what it felt like to wake up next to Michael there. She will exist in an empty place.

"Everything okay, honey?" Michael asks, knowing full well that she is not okay. If I can see it, he certainly can.

"Everything is as fine as it's going to be." Rachel makes a hard line with her lips and pats Michael's hand.

"Can I see those?" Michael points to the papers in Rachel's hand and then takes them from her without waiting for her reply. His eyes turn into saucers and he blows hard the breath that he held for the five seconds it took him to see what was so shocking.

Rachel takes the papers from him and folds them over, shoving them in her purse.

"We'll look at those later," she says.

Michael takes in the desolate look on Rachel's face. The impact it has on him is visible on his own. I can imagine they've shed plenty of tears in the last eight months just dealing with his terminal diagnosis. No one wants to talk about the logistics of dying, but it has to be done. Unfortunately, those logistics include figuring out how all the bills are going to be paid.

"We … we have a good savings and some investments. And, we were already talking about selling the business to one of my pilots. Between those things, Rachel is going to be just fine." Michael looks at Rachel and squeezes her hand. "But, honestly, I can't bear the thought of her getting rid of her family's land."

"Michael, it's okay," Rachel protests.

"It's not okay. And it's not right that I even entertained the thought." He looks at Will and steels himself. "If your offer still stands."

"It absolutely still stands … with one condition," Will tells him.

"Anything," Michael replies.

"You give us a chance to be brothers." My heart is beating like a full on drum corps inside my chest. It's one thing for Michael to humble himself and accept our help for Rachel's sake. It's another to tear down the wall he built and let Will in. I don't know what Will is going to do if Michael says 'no.'

Michael is not quick to reply. I can almost see the wheels turning in his head as he contemplates how he wants to spend his last days.

"There was a time I knew I could never even think about that. I was convinced you were just like him and I didn't want any part of that. But, you were there tonight for us, and that says a lot about who you are as a man. So, I guess it's time I got to know my little brother."

Will breathes a sigh of relief and the room practically glows from the smiles beaming from our faces. And while Michael's prognosis isn't good, we know that we are about to embark on a short but marvelous road.

Chapter 7

Cancer sucks and I want to punch it in the face.

In the last three weeks, Michael has had three more episodes like the one at our house. If he would keep himself hydrated like his doctors have told him to, this wouldn't keep happening. Now that he has begun a relationship with us, Rachel is happy to have more people staying on top of Michael about this. And when Michael's mother, Victoria, heard that Michael had knocked down the wall he had up between him and Will, she was ecstatic. It was killing her not to tell us what was going on with Michael, but he had given her strict instructions not to share their personal issues with us. I think it's the only reason she hasn't already come to see him. She knows that this is truly the only time Michael and Will are ever going to have together.

"Are you all packed?" Will asks, entering our bedroom with a baby in each arm.

"I am, but I'm still not sure about this." I take Natalie from his arms and hold her close to me. "I know it's only two nights, but I've never been away from them before."

In a few short hours I will be boarding a plane to New York to ambush Caroline and get things straight between us. We haven't spoken since the night she stormed out, which was almost month ago. I've tried to reach her countless times since that night at dinner, but she won't reply to any of my calls, emails, or texts. When her own mother couldn't get her to call me back, I decided that desperate times definitely called for desperate measures. Carol was more than willing to oblige in helping me figure out what was going on with Caroline. So she gave me the spare key to Caroline's apartment in New York and I booked my flight.

"It's going to be fine. I'm here and the moms are chomping at the bit to come help out tonight." Will envelops me in his arms and I rest my head on his strong chest, letting the nervousness in me calm.

"I'm sure you're right. But just to make myself feel better…" I pull a folded piece of paper from my nightstand and hand it to Will. "I've detailed the girls' day and made some notes."

"You do remember that I've been here most days since they were born, right?"

"I said it was to make *myself* feel better." I look up at Will with doe eyes and grin.

"You are way too cute for your own good. You know that, don't you?"

"And you love me for it!" I wrap my arms around Will's middle and he kisses me on the top of my head.

"Yes, yes I do." Will grabs my small suitcase from the bed just as the doorbell rings. "That must be Tyler. He said he wanted to stop by before you left."

When we open the door, Tyler is standing there looking a little beaten. The last time we asked him about Caroline he said that they were speaking but that things definitely felt off. She suggested that maybe they should break up, but Tyler said that wasn't happening and Caroline hasn't mentioned it again. He hasn't seen her since that night at our house and it's beginning to wear on him.

"Hey," I say, giving Tyler a hug when he walks in.

"Hey. You all set?" he asks and I nod in reply.

"Have you talked to her lately?" I ask him. "What's she saying?"

"Yeah, I talked to her yesterday. She says that we're fine but she won't talk about Europe. She's supposed to be leaving in a month and she won't talk to me about it. She just tells me that I don't need to worry, but how am I supposed to not worry when she won't talk to me?"

I don't think I've ever seen Tyler this upset and rambling before. I also don't think that any girl he's dated has ever been as important to him as Caroline is.

"I was going to ask her to marry me. I still want to. I just don't know if she feels the same way anymore."

"Well, I'm going to do everything I can to find out what's going on. It isn't like Caroline to act this way, and there's too much at stake for me to let it go."

Tyler hangs out for a bit until it's time for Will to take me to the airport. He insists on parking and staying with me until I'm checked in and am ready to go through security.

"I've arranged for a car to pick you up at the airport and stay available to you all weekend. You've got enough to handle without having to deal with New York City cabbies," Will tells me.

"You're too sweet." A car service is unnecessary but I learned a long time ago not to argue points of chivalry and care with Will.

Will kisses me and then I kiss my sweet little munchkins before I leave them at the entrance to the security checkpoint. Once my shoes are back on, I wave and blow a kiss to him from across the cluster of people waiting their turn in the full body-scan machine.

I run through my plan of action before my flight while I snack on my chai tea latte and petite vanilla scones from Starbucks. Carol wasn't sure of Caroline's schedule since it could literally run from first thing in the morning until the wee hours of the night. So if she isn't at her apartment, I'll just use the key Carol gave me and let myself in. I'll turn all the lights on so when Caroline does get home, she'll know something is up when she walks in.

The driver Will promised would be waiting for me in Baggage Claim is holding a sign with "Mrs. Layla Meyer" printed on it. I'm reminded of when we arrived at this same airport on the first leg of our honeymoon. It was the first time I had seen my married name printed and I was overwhelmed with emotion. Funny how it still does the same thing to me now.

I tell the driver that I'll call the service when I'm ready for them to pick me up. I have a hotel reserved, but I'm willing to wait all night to talk to Caroline if I have to. I knock on her door and no one answers. It's almost six, but Caroline keeps anything but typical work hours.

"Hellooooo!" I call as I open the door. Nope. No one here.

Sleek white furniture lines a pink and green floral carpet in the middle of the room, with crisp, white and pink pillows on both the couch and loveseat. Pink, blue, and green accent pieces are strategically placed on a bookshelf with all of Caroline's favorite books. Some of them are stacked with a vase or trinket on top. The place is beautiful, but much more sterile than I would have thought. But since Caroline divides her time between here and Los Angeles, it's probably hard to personalize the space as much as she'd like.

A search for something to eat in the kitchen turns up a jug of orange juice and a loaf of bread. I'm not surprised. Caroline isn't much of a cook. I do find an abundance of take-out menus. All of Caroline's favorite dishes are circled. I place an order for Chinese, being sure to include something for Caroline, and wait. It only takes twenty minutes for them to arrive, which is about twenty minutes less than what we wait at home. When I ask the delivery guy how he was able to get here so quickly, he tells me that they are just a block away, and that they are *very* familiar with this address.

"I bet you are!" I laugh as I put his tip in his hand.

I leave everything in the thick, brown grocery bag and set it on the counter. I'm hoping Caroline will be home soon and we can talk while we eat together. It would be like old times.

I walk down the hallway, passing a bedroom and bathroom before finding Caroline's bedroom. A soft smile turns up the corners of my mouth. Caroline's room is every bit of what I thought it would be. A queen-size sleigh bed made out of warm mahogany sits centered on the wall to the right. The quilt her grandmother made for her is neatly made over the mattress. And the lamp we bought together when Ikea opened in Charlotte is sitting on her nightstand. The matching dresser opposite the bed is covered with framed pictures. I take a few steps into the room so I can examine them more closely. That small smile I had turns into a full on, face-splitting grin. Every frame is filled with pictures of our group, our family. There's one with Caroline, Gwen, and me from prom, another of all of us from that first trip to Grandfather Mountain, and another one from graduation. And while there are several from random events and selfies, the one that sits centered on the dresser in the largest frame is my favorite. It is of Caroline and me on my wedding day. I pick the frame up and become even more determined to get Caroline and me back to where we used to be.

"Hey." Caroline's voice startles me. I didn't hear the door or her footsteps in the hall. I spin around, the frame still in my hand.

"Hi," I say with a surprised jolt. I realize I'm still holding the frame and turn quickly to put it back in its place.

"I knew I hadn't left all the lights on. I saw your suitcase and purse, but the smell of Chinese food would have been enough to tell me you were here." She tosses her coat and scarf onto the bed and kicks her shoes off into the middle of the room before turning back to me. "What are you doing here, Layla?"

"You wouldn't return any of my calls, texts, or emails. You mom gave me her spare key," I tell her. "We need to talk. I don't like how things were left. I mean, it's been a month since we've spoken."

Caroline lets out a defeated breath. She knows she is trapped. There's no way I'm leaving here without things getting cleared up.

"Well, what do you want to drink?"

"You have nothing in your fridge," I remind her as we walk down the hall to the kitchen. I pull two plates from the cabinet Caroline directs me to and begin serving our dinner.

"You didn't look in the right place," she tells me. I watch as Caroline gets down on her knees and pulls two six packs of soda out from the back of the cabinet. "I can't leave this in my fridge. The other designers give me a hard time. Everyone here is like, 'I'll have a chardonnay and the salmon' and I'm all 'can't I just get some Chinese food and a Cheerwine?'"

I laugh and make a face because that pretty well sums up dining with Caroline. We smile and laugh with each other, and the hope I had at resolving whatever it is that has come between us is stronger than ever.

We're a few bites in when I have to dive right in. "You want to tell me what that scene at my house was?"

"I don't know. I don't know what came over me. I'm sorry I acted that way. I shouldn't have said those things to you." Caroline twists her mouth in contemplation.

"What about Tyler? I don't understand why you would drop that kind of bomb on him in front of everyone. And how can you just decide that you're going to go to Europe indefinitely without talking to him?"

"You don't understand. I meant it when I said that not everyone gets a fairy tale romance like you and Will. How is anyone supposed to compete with that?"

"Why are you trying to compete?" I give her a puzzled look. "I wouldn't wish Will's and my journey on my worst enemy. I'm so glad we landed where we did, but the steps we took to get here were awful. You know that, Care. And even if Will and I hadn't found our happy ending, you still have your parents' example. I don't know much about Tyler's parents, but they seem pretty happy."

Caroline stands and refills her glass from the remaining soda in the can. "But what about my mother—I mean, my birth mom? She was a prostitute. She didn't know the meaning of love. For God's sake, Layla, she didn't even know who my father was! She got pregnant from some trick because condoms are only ninety-nine point nine percent effective!"

"What do her choices have to do with you?" I meet her at the counter.

"What if I'm predestined to—" she begins but I have to cut her off there.

"What is it with people thinking that genetics have something to do with the choices we make?" I shake my head, as I am growing weary of hearing this crap.

"Look at you. Your parents were strong and determined, and that's exactly how you turned out!" she argues.

"Yes. They had strong and determined personalities, but they could have made any number of choices with those traits. You'll remember that my father chose to blow up a building in protest. Take Will's father for example. He was a brilliant businessman. He chose to take those skills and use them for evil, destroying who knows how many lives." I take Caroline by the shoulders, rubbing them to comfort her. "Why are you so scared?"

"I love him, Layla. I've never loved anyone the way I love Tyler. Actually, I don't think I've ever been in love with anyone … ever. I'm so scared that I'm going to do something that is going to push him away forever," she says as her salty tears finally escape down her face.

"So you decided to push him away intentionally?"

"I guess I just wanted to see what he would do. I mean, if I did something really inconsiderate and selfish, would he stick around? Would he love me through it?" Caroline's sobs come harder and she falls to the floor. I go there with her and hold my best friend in my arms while she cries. "But now I've ruined everything!"

"Shh," I whisper as I stroke her hair. "You haven't ruined anything. Tyler is mad about you. He wants to marry you."

Caroline snaps her head up. "He does?" she says with shock. "You mean he *wanted* to marry me."

"Why can't you just accept that he loves you? That even though you were a total bitch to us that night, we *both* still love you?" I smirk at her and she laughs.

"Oh, Layla! I'm so sorry!" Caroline wraps her arms around my neck and we settle our reconciliation with a long embrace on her kitchen floor.

"Are you really going to Europe for an undetermined amount of time?" I ask Caroline as we make ourselves comfortable on her bed. We caught up on her life during dinner and I bombarded her with pictures of the twins for almost an hour. Now we've decided it's ice cream and movie night, just like we used to do on our famous girls' nights. It makes me miss Gwen.

"I could if I wanted to. They really want me to lead several projects over there," she says with a sigh.

"Then I guess the real question is, do you want to?" I dip my spoon into her ice cream carton and take a bit of chocolate chunk, staring at her while I wait for her answer.

"I do. But, I want to be with Tyler, too." She thinks for a moment before become resolute. "I can't lose him, Layla. I just can't. I'll make it work. I'll … I'll commit to two full weeks of non-stop work and one full week home. And I'll … I'll master the art of delegation. Can you teach me how not to be a control freak?" She laughs nervously and I laugh with her.

"Of course!"

"Then it's settled." Caroline's tone is determined. "I'm going to ask Tyler to marry me!"

"Wait. What?" Her declaration practically knocks me off the bed. "Are you sure you want to do that?"

"Yes! I love him and I know he loves me. Besides, it's the twenty-first century. Why can't I be the one to ask? And it will let him know that I'm all in." She's so excited that I don't want to be a buzz kill. I just want her to really think about this.

"No, definitely, yeah!" I say. "It's just … well, is that the fairy tale you want? Is that going to be the romantic story you want to tell your kids one day?"

"Every love story is different." She smiles at me. I know she is right and I can't help but smile back at her.

"Okay. If that's what you want. Then I'm going to make sure you have the most amazing engagement anyone has ever had!"

I cancel my reservation at the hotel and Caroline and I spend the rest of the night watching chick flicks and eating junk food. With every bite I know Wes is going to kick my ass even harder. I tell her about Michael and she shares the same conflicted feelings I have. Will and I are so happy to have Michael and Rachel in our lives, but our time with Michael is so short. Every day Michael will get a little weaker and we know it's just a matter of time before he will leave us.

We also talk about some ideas for her Sadie Hawkins proposal to Tyler. Everything she suggests sounds wonderful, but this whole non-traditional approach just isn't sitting right with me. Deep down, I think she'll regret it one day. Since she's asked for my help in executing what she is calling "The Proposal of the Century," I tell her I'm going to need some time to make sure Michael is in a stable place. She agrees and I have just bought some time to see if I can make good on my promise of making sure she gets the Happily Ever After she deserves.

Chapter 8

Caroline called in a favor with her boss and took the next day off. We slept in but I called Will as soon as my eyes were focused enough to see the numbers on my phone. I was frantically apologetic, feeling guilty for having enjoyed my long, uninterrupted night of slumber so much. He told me to stop apologizing and to enjoy my time with Caroline. He said the girls were just fine, and he was actually really enjoying having them all to himself. He planned for Michael to come over that night to play poker. It made me so happy to hear that he and Will were truly taking advantage of the time Michael has left.

We shopped all day. I bought the girls dresses for their baptisms and a few toys from FAO Schwarz. I'd never spent so much on them, but Caroline told me to get used to it. She was just sorry that they wouldn't be old enough to be flower girls in her wedding. I suggested that she plan the wedding far enough out so that maybe they could crawl down the aisle but that was a No-Go.

When Will picks me up at the airport he's quiet. Unusually quiet.

I get in the car and close the car door beside me. "What's wrong?"

"It's Michael," he says.

"What happened?"

"He's been pushing through and not telling me how he's been doing. He's fading, Layla. I mean, I noticed he was looking bad, but I had no idea just how bad he was really doing. He had another episode last night. I had to call an ambulance again." Will grips the steering wheel, trying not to cry.

"I'm so sorry I wasn't here," I tell him. I put my hand on his leg and then rub his knee. "I should have been here."

"No. You should have been in New York talking some sense into your best girlfriend. There was nothing here you could have done."

"So are we going to the hospital right now?" I'm all for going if that's what Will needs, but I really want to go home and see my babies, if I can pry them out of my mother's hands.

"Let's go home so you can see the girls. I'll call Rachel and see how Michael is doing." Will blows out a breath of hard air. "It's happening too fast. I knew we had limited time, but it's dwindling away so quickly."

"Just keep making the most of the time you have with him. And when he's gone, you'll have these memories. They'll all be so fresh that you won't forget anything." I rub Will's leg again to comfort him. He takes my hand in his and rests it on his thigh. We are quiet the rest of the drive home.

Mom must have seen us pull in the driveway because she is standing in the foyer with both Natalie and Claire in her arms.

"Mommy's home!" she says in a sweet, high-pitched voice. The girls giggle and I literally drop my purse on the floor and rush to them.

"Oh my goodness! You grew in two days!" I take Claire from her and kiss her sweet cheeks. She puts Natalie in my other arm and I alternate kisses between my two little cherubs.

Luke enters from the study. "Well, I guess our Grammy and Papa time is over." He smiles at me and my heart swells. I love watching the two of them with my girls. It feels redemptive in a way. Being grandparents in their forties means that they'll get to watch Natalie and Claire grow up the way they never got to with Penny.

Will finally walks through the front door. I left him in the car so he could call Rachel and get an update on Michael. I only caught the front end of their conversation, which involved Will's very sad eyes, a "really," and an "are you sure."

"Maybe not, if that's okay with you." Will touches the small of my back and then takes Natalie from me. "Apparently Michael's cancer is spreading faster now. It's so rapid that his doctors are suggesting he go home and make himself comfortable. It could be just a matter of a few weeks now. So, I want, no … I need to be out there with him as much as possible. And Rachel could use Layla's company."

"Of course," I agree.

"We'll do everything we can to help," Dad offers. "And I'm sure Wes and Eliana will, too."

Mom helps me whip some dinner together while Dad spends time with Will. He knows better than anyone what Will is going through. He may have just gotten Michael, but the way Will commits and loves so completely, it doesn't matter that they accepted their brotherhood less than a couple of months ago. Will's brother is dying and it is tearing him apart.

I remember Dad telling me that it didn't matter that he and my father weren't close when he died. Family is family and the sadness can be overwhelming. Dad was sad for having lost all those years with my father. Will feels the same way about the lost years with Michael. The difference in their experiences is that Michael will have Will by his side when he passes. He will leave this earth with more love than when he entered it. I hope that Will is able to find solace in that.

"How is Victoria dealing with all of this?" Luke asks. "Losing a child is devastating. To watch him deteriorate must be heartbreaking."

"I've only spoken to her once," Will tells him. "She's doing as well as can be expected, but our reconciliation seemed to make her feel better. She's been telling him for years to connect with me but he's pretty stubborn." Will thinks for a moment. "It's funny. After getting to know Michael and the girls, it seems we all inherited that trait from our father."

"Do you ever think that there might be some traits of his that wouldn't be so bad to have?" I ask. Gregory Meyer was a ruthless and evil man, that isn't up for debate. But no one starts out as pure evil. He had qualities and characteristics that he chose to use in a malicious way. He could have just as easily used them charitably.

"I try not to think about my father all that much." Will stands and takes his plate to the kitchen. I can't tell if he's angry or just avoiding the subject.

I raise my eyebrows at Mom and follow him. "I didn't mean to upset you."

"You didn't."

"Then what's up with the physical relocation?" I give him the look that reminds him that I know him better than anyone.

"I meant what I said, Layla. I try not to think about my father. There isn't a lot worth remembering." Will busies himself with loading the dishwasher. After a few plates and two glasses he stops and positions his hands wide apart on the edge of the counter and hangs his head. "It's all his fault."

I knew exactly what he means. It was all Gregory Meyer's fault that Will and Michael didn't have a relationship until now. Had he allowed Eliana to contact the ex-wives and make connections between Will and his half-siblings, Will and Michael wouldn't have been strangers. But that wouldn't have been very Gregory Meyer of him.

"I'm sorry. I didn't mean to stir any of that up." I snake my body in front of Will's and lean against the counter. He lifts his head and then wraps his arms around me.

"It's okay. I said I *try* not to think about him. Lately it's been difficult. Every time we tell a story about something Michael and I both experienced at a certain age, all I can think is that it would have been really nice to have an experienced older brother help me through it. And then I just get pissed. I'm really happy to have Michael in my life, but it's been hard dealing with the feelings it's dredged up."

"Well, I'm still sorry. I shouldn't have asked such a stupid question." I squeeze my arms around Will's middle in apology.

"It wasn't a stupid question. It was a normal question. The problem is, my father was never normal."

Mom and Dad peek around the corner before walking into the

kitchen. "Everything okay in here?" Mom asks.

"We're good," Will tells her. "Thanks for staying. I appreciate the talk, Luke."

"Anytime." Luke gives a hard pat to Will's back before grabbing his shoulder. "I'm always here for you."

Mom and Dad are more than agreeable to being on-call to watch the twins in the coming weeks. We don't know how fast Michael is going to continue to fade, but Will wants to be there with him as much as possible, and that's exactly what we're going to do.

We've already made arrangements with the hospital and Michael's doctors to have all of his bills sent to us. Will even went as far as to have a meal delivery subscription set up for Rachel, for which she is very grateful. She said that she wants to keep things as normal as possible. Cooking is one normal thing that she loves to do, but is happy to not have to deal with the grocery store. She doesn't like to be away from Michael too long, and with everything going on it's hard to concentrate long enough to get through the entire store.

Silence fills most of our time at home over the coming days. It isn't awkward or strange. It is a respectful silence. The kind that understands that there are no words that could possibly encompass the feelings Will is dealing with. He is reliving so much of the pain that his father inflicted upon him and Michael, as well as their half-sisters, through his act of abandonment. The silence also comes because Will is also using most of his daily word allotment with Michael. When Michael is here at the house, Will won't shut up. He's cramming in a lifetime of conversations each day because we don't know what tomorrow will bring.

We're so grateful that Will has such good guys working for him, too. They gladly took on some extra work and responsibilities when Will cut down his time in the shop when the babies were born. He's in the shop even less these days, giving as much of his free time to Michael as possible. It's meant so much to us that Will gave them all a hefty bonus in their last checks.

"So … we haven't talked in a while. How are you?" I climb into bed next to Will and he welcomes me under his arm. I rest my head on his chest and sigh. In spite of all the sadness that seems to be lingering around us right now, this is always my happiest, sweetest spot.

"Today was a hard day," he says.

"Michael's going fast, isn't he?"

"Yeah, but watching him waste away wasn't the only difficult thing today. His birthday is next month."

"Oh." I immediately realize where Will is going.

"I just got my brother and I'm not even going to get to celebrate a birthday with him."

"I'm sorry, babe. That sucks." I push myself up and nuzzle Will's neck before kissing his cheek. We lie there together in quiet contemplation. Will strokes my arm gently, inviting a gaggle of goose bumps to rise with each pass. All I can think is that I wish Will had more time with him. Just one more year to celebrate his birthday and every important holiday is all I'm asking for.

"I have an ambitious idea." I sit up and turn to face Will. Seeing the look on my face, Will shimmies himself up and leans against his pillow on the headboard awaiting my announcement. "Who says we can't celebrate his birthday now? In fact, who says we can't celebrate every holiday that we're going to miss with him now?" I raise my eyebrows in anticipation of Will's reply.

"What are you talking about?" His face is scrunched together in confusion.

"Let's give him a birthday party. Let's have Christmas, and Thanksgiving, and Easter! Hell, let's celebrate Arbor Day! The point is there is nothing that says we have to wait until those actual days to celebrate. We can have a whole day that celebrates every holiday we aren't going to get with him."

Will sits up and looks me square in the eye. "You are the most brilliant woman on the planet. God, I'm so glad you're mine!" He pulls me to him and kisses me hard. "Seriously, babe, that is the best idea I've ever heard."

"Okay," I begin as the wheels start really turning. "I'm going to need the moms' help. I'll see if Carol can watch the girls while Mom, Eliana and I go shopping. You said Michael has a doctor appointment on Wednesday morning, right?" Will nods as he follows along. "Great! That gives us a day to shop. We won't have much time on Wednesday, but if you take him to the appointment then we should be able to get to their house and decorate."

"Do you think Rachel will go for it?"

"I think she's going to bawl her eyes out with joy over it!"

Sleep evades us most of the night because excitement has taken residence in its place. We doze off for a bit, and then one of us will say, "Are you awake?" in a hushed tone. To which the other one always says, "Yes, and I have another idea."

I texted both Mom and Eliana in the night and told them our idea. Mom's text reply came almost immediately. Eliana's comes just before sunrise. I have to force myself to wait until the sun is fully up before I call Rachel. When I tell her our plan, she is overwhelmed with joy and agrees to everything I suggest. Carol is a lifesaver and agrees to watch the girls while the moms and I go shopping for everything we need. Between food, gifts, and the perfect decorations for our day of celebrating, it's a lot. We hit five different stores and call a rental company for the pipe and draping we need. They charge us an arm and a leg for the last minute rental, but it's going to be totally worth it to see the look on Michael's face.

We split up and each head to our attics for the holiday decorations we're going to need and then reconvene back at my house. We spend hours sorting through everything and making a master plan. Rachel and I will do all the cooking while Mom and Eliana decorate. It's going to be perfect!

It's early, just after seven, when Mom, Eliana, and I follow Will all the way to Michael's. We pull up to the next road and keep an eye out for them to leave the dirt road for the paved one and head in the direction of Michael's doctor. We have to be quick. We've only got a few hours before Carol is going to bring the twins and Will returns with Michael.

I knock excitedly on the storm door and it takes only seconds before Rachel is answering. "Hey!" I squeal.

"I can't believe you're doing this!" she says, tears forming in her eyes.

"I'm just glad you agreed." We hug and she helps haul everything into the house just as the rental people arrive with the pipe and drape.

"What's that for?" Rachel's face is a mixture of confusion and joy. Her eyebrows are furrowed together and her smile is so big that her cheeks are making her eyes disappear.

"You'll see!" I say cryptically. "So, not that it matters, but do you think he's going to love or hate this?"

"Well, he loves holidays but hates birthday parties. So it's kind of a crap shoot."

"Perfect!"

Will texts me when they are leaving the hospital, giving us our one-hour countdown, so I call Carol to bring the girls. It wouldn't be a family celebration without them, and Michael and Rachel have formed a sweet bond with them already.

"Wow. I can't believe what we accomplished in three hours." Rachel covers her mouth as we walk from room to room surveying the transformation each space has taken. "Thank you so much for this, all of you." Tears begin to stream down Rachel's face. I can only imagine the mix of emotions she is feeling. How would I feel if the love of my life were slipping away right before me? What would I think as I knew our days were numbered? When would I stop being able to hold it together all the time and just collapse?

The food for our first course, Christmas brunch, is warming in the oven while Eliana—a.k.a. the best mother-in-law on the planet—holds down the fort in the kitchen prepping for our Thanksgiving feast to come this evening.

Will pulls into the space next to my car, and I can imagine Michael asking what I'm doing here, to which Will gives him a vague answer about their wives becoming wonderful friends. We all stand in the large entry with party hats on our heads, and streamers and silly string at the ready. Rachel is beaming and all the excitement is about to explode from inside her.

The storm door creaks open and we all hold a collective breath in anticipation. Michael's feet have barely crossed the threshold when we can't hold it in any longer.

"SURPRISE!" Our voices are so loud that they echo through the whole house.

Michael is stunned, to say the least. It's a good thing Will is right behind him because he takes a step backward as our celebratory shouts knock him over.

"What's going on here?" He laughs.

"This is your surprise birthday party, honey!" Rachel says. She throws her arms gingerly around him and kisses him sweetly. He is weak, and becoming frailer every day, so she is gentle with him.

"But my birthday …" he begins.

"We don't care when your actual birthday is. We're not going to let time deter us from sharing life's most important celebrations with you." Will drapes his arm over Michael and smiles. "I get to have one birthday with my big brother."

Michael is moved. If his complexion were not so pale, he may have been able to hide his struggle to hold back the tears that want to cascade down his face.

He swallows hard. "This is amazing. Thank you."

It's a big deal for him to give into the moment and just say "thank you." This time developing a relationship with us has broken Michael's pride as he's allowed us in.

We settle in the front room where a cake and gifts are waiting. Will helps Michael sit in his favorite wing back chair. A family heirloom, it was Rachel's grandfather's and has been passed down to each generation. Before we go any further, Michael tells us the beautiful story of when Rachel's father gave it to him before he passed. He lay dying in his room upstairs and used some of his last breaths to tell Michael how much he meant to him, and that it would mean the world to him if he would take the chair as his own, and one day pass it along to his son.

"Will … I want you to have the chair," Michael says softly.

"Oh, Michael, are you sure? Wouldn't it mean more for Rachel to keep it?" Will replies.

"She hates this damn thing!" He laughs. "One day you and Layla may have a son, and I want you to pass it down to him."

"Well, only if it's okay with Rachel."

"Oh, for the love of all that is holy, please take the chair!" Rachel laughs.

Will echoes her laugh. "Okay then! Looks like we've got a new chair coming to us!"

Michael is just about to blow out the candle on his cake when Carol arrives with Natalie and Claire.

"There they are!" Will says, meeting Carol at the door and relieving her of one of the car-seat carriers. The girls are dressed in the sweetest pink party dresses, white ruffled socks, and pink patent shoes.

"This must be a magical candle to grant me my wish before I even blow it out," Michael says, beaming. "I was afraid my birthday celebration wasn't going to include the most beautiful girls in the world!"

He sits back in the chair and we put both girls in his arms. It's beautiful and sad to watch him with them. He and Rachel wanted to have children but it never happened. And then when he got sick, the possibility of becoming parents was destroyed.

I pull my phone out and take a dozen shots to add to the growing collection of pictures of Michael and our new family. Carol stays and takes several pictures of all of us together before heading back to the kitchen to help Eliana.

We eat cake and Michael opens his gifts, laughing at the "old" gag gifts Will got him. "I'm only thirty-eight, man!" he'd say. He loves the blanket I found for him. It's a patchwork of old sweaters stitched together with a warm lining. He gets cold pretty easily these days.

His last gift is really for both him and Rachel. It's an album of pictures I've been taking over the last months. There are pictures of Michael and the girls, him and Will, and all of us together. Some are staged but a lot of them are candid pictures he didn't know I was taking. Those are my favorite pictures, as they show the light and joy in Michael's eyes, even when his body started taking a turn for the worse.

"This is beautiful," Michael says through the tears he isn't even remotely trying to hide. "I love it. *We* love it." He takes Rachel's hand

and kisses it.

"So," he says, collecting himself. "If I recall that whirlwind of an entrance earlier, you said something about celebrating life's most important *celebrations*. Plural. What else do you have up your sleeves? And … do I smell a turkey?"

"Well, Mr. Meadows, we do have a few more surprises for you," I say with a snicker. I'm giddy with anticipation.

"Uh oh!" he exclaims.

Will helps Michael up from his seat and escorts him to the family room. There is a pipe and draping shielding the room from view. Michael cocks an eyebrow up and looks at me suspiciously with a smile.

"And what, exactly, is behind door number two?"

"I hope you're ready for this," I warn. With that, I pull the draping aside and reveal a Christmas winter wonderland. A seven-foot tree is fully decorated in the corner of the room with a train and track encircling it. Icicle lights trim the perimeter of the ceiling and an entire Christmas village has taken residence on the top of the baby grand piano in the bay window. And presents. Lots of presents are under the tree for all of us. Rachel was so excited about the presents that she was able to sneak out yesterday and buy a few from them to us. I told her she didn't have to do that, but she insisted participating in the gift giving.

Leaning against Will, Michael covers his mouth with both hands in utter shock. I look at Will, feeling accomplished in creating a day that is already full of love and joy. A day that none of us will ever forget. A day full of memories that will trump the sad ones upon us.

Will holds back his own tears as he looks at Michael. "Merry Christmas, brother."

Chapter 9

We were gifted eleven more days with Michael before he passed.

Four days after the day we celebrated Michael's birthday, Christmas, and Thanksgiving, he took a turn for the worse. We brought Hospice in to help, as each day was touch and go. Will pretty much moved in and spent every waking hour, and then some, by Michael's side. He read Michael's favorite books aloud to him and helped feed him what little he could keep down. Eventually Michael stopped eating altogether because his body just couldn't process anything. His mother, Victoria, was there for his last three days on this earth.

Michael took his last breath at two thirty-seven on a Thursday afternoon with his wife, his mother, his brother, and me by his side. It was an emotional day for all of us, but the worst day of Rachel's life. She lost her best friend and partner. She saw it coming and there was nothing she could do but wait for it to happen.

Will and Michael's sisters came in for the funeral. It was the first time they had all been together since our wedding. Not exactly the reunion they were hoping for, but all agreed it was nice to see each other.

Funerals are strange for me. They bring on a mix of emotions due to my only points of reference for them: my parents' funeral where I wasn't allowed to speak, my grandmother's funeral where everyone should be glad I didn't speak, my grandfather's funeral where my too-young self gave the eulogy, and Will's funeral where his father gave an Oscar-worthy performance. Michael's funeral, I've decided, is going to erase all of the other funeral memories. Will turned it into a day to celebrate Michael's life. A day when the life and character of his brother was the focus, not his sad and too-early departure.

Victoria stayed with Rachel for a week as we all helped her pack Michael's things up. I asked if she wanted to wait a bit, but she said that Michael asked her not to and she wanted to honor his request. Victoria and I followed her instructions on what was staying and what was going, which was most of it. She kept pictures and a knick-knack or two, a few of Michael's favorite t-shirts, and the blanket we gave him for his birthday. Other than that, everything else of his went.

The whole thing was devastating for Will. He worked directly with the funeral director to lessen the burden on Rachel. He spent two days preparing his eulogy for the service and kept such a brave face with every word.

We hosted a reception at our house for friends and what little family Michael had left. Outside of Rachel, the only family Michael had was his mother, Will, and their sisters. The people who worked for Michael had a lot of respect for him. We met Clive, the guy who is buying the hot air balloon company, and he seemed like he was really invested in making it work. Will didn't like the idea of the business ever going under, so he made Clive promise to come to Will if there were any financial problems. Will felt like it was his responsibility to keep that legacy alive.

After the reception was over, and the dust settled from all the waiting and planning and carrying out of plans, Will and I collapsed on our bed, physically and emotionally exhausted. That was when, once again, I held my husband while he wept for the loss of his brother.

We cuddled the girls a lot in the days that followed. It amazes me the impact death has on a person. The impact it has had on me in my life. But watching the impact it has had on Will has been the most upsetting. The last thing I ever want him or the girls to experience is pain. I know I can't keep it from them. And I suppose I'm not sure I would if I were able to. I have learned that pain can be a necessary catalyst to growth. But, to be honest, I'm having a hard time seeing the growth potential from this experience.

With Michael's death behind us, we begin to look ahead at life. New life. Specifically, the life Tyler and Caroline want to have together. I had only a couple of conversations with Caroline during Michael's final days and in the month that followed. She wanted to be sure I cleared my calendar for the days she was going to sneak into town to plan her epic proposal. Those conversations were silver linings to the otherwise dark clouds that seemed to surround me at the time.

Caroline is going to be here in twenty minutes, so I have to shove Will out the door or everything will be ruined. Eliana is coming in thirty minutes to watch the girls and then we'll be on our way.

"You're sure you can handle this today?" I ask Will. "It's the first time you've been out there since …"

"I'm fine, Layla." Will kisses the top of my head. "But I appreciate your concern. This is actually just what I need."

I let out a relieved sigh. "Good … now leave!"

"Geez! Alright already!" he laughs. "Is there anything else I need to do besides get the groom-to-be there?"

"No. Rachel said she has everything covered on their end. And from what she's described, it's going to be ridiculous!" I wrap my arms around Will's middle, remembering the Christmas night he proposed to me on the dock in Tallahassee. Despite the craziness of the life we were living at the time, it was the most perfect proposal I could have ever dreamed of. "Oh, and I got a text from her this morning confirming that the weather is more than ideal for today."

"Awesome! Okay … I think I have everything. Let me get out of here before Caroline arrives." I open the front door for Will and he kisses me hard. "You know … I'm thinking all this romance is going to set the mood for later, if you know what I mean." I love the seductively sinister grin of my husband.

"Oh, I know exactly what you mean and I've already thought ahead." I give him a sexy smile and kiss him so he knows I mean business.

"I've said it before, and I'll say it again: Best. Wife. Ever."

"I know. Now go! I'll see you soon. Love you!"

"Love you, too, babe!"

I watch Will until his car disappears and then go inside to finalize everything. I feed the girls and get little bags of snacks prepared for them along with their dinner so Gramma Ellie doesn't have to worry about it.

The doorbell rings and I practically jump out of my skin. I'm so excited and nervous, which is crazy because today is totally not about me.

"Hey, you!" I say to Caroline. She crosses the threshold and hugs me fiercely.

"Hey! I've missed you! Today is going to be so fun!"

"It's going to be the best!" I tell her. If she only knew! "We have to multitask a bit, though. I hope that's okay."

"Sure, what's up? Something with my girls?" Caroline hears the babbles of Natalie and Claire and makes a beeline for the back room where the girls are laughing with each other in their play yard. Unable to resist, Caroline picks Claire up and smothers her with kisses.

"No, actually. Eliana is on her way over to watch them for me. Will has some business out at Rachel's and he left something here that he needs. Some file or something that he says he left in my car." That seemed like the most plausible lie we could tell her. "So, we're going to have to take the first part of our planning session on the road."

"Oh, that's cool. You drive, I'll talk!"

Within minutes Eliana is there and mostly ignoring me, as happens when the grandparents get around these two girls. She's been helpful enough that I don't have to do anything to prep her except point to which food item comes next.

We get in the car and are part way down the road when Caroline's wardrobe choice finally registers with me.

"What are you wearing?" I say.

"What?"

"What is that on your shirt?"

"Um … it's Barbie. You know, the silhouette logo of the iconic doll." Her tone is sarcastic and confused. "You don't like Barbie, or something?"

"No, I love Barbie," I tell her. I need to think. Do I fake a gas stop and text Rachel to see if she has something Caroline can wear, or do we let this day be captured for all eternity with Caroline wearing a *Barbie* t-shirt?

I take the ramp onto the highway and round the sharp curve into the merge lane when we hear a thud from the back of the car.

"What was that?" Caroline turns around in her seat looking for the source of our startle. That's when I find the solution to the impending problem.

"That's a box of clothes I'm taking to the Help Center. Some stuff that doesn't fit any of us anymore, and a few things I just don't wear." I remember now that there is a black and red houndstooth, thigh-length trench coat in that box that Caroline mentioned liking. It will work perfectly!

"Oh, well that's good. I thought you were hiding a body back there or something," she laughs. "So … here's what I'm thinking. You know how Tyler loves paintball?" I nod and wonder where in the world she is going with this. Paintball does not scream *romantic proposal*. "Well, I was thinking Will could get the guys together and they could go play paintball during one of the open-play times. They do this thing where you don't have to be part of a group. It's kind of a free-for-all. When enough people are there, they play an every-man-for-himself game."

Paintball? Really? "Okay. So how does the proposal fit into that very non-romantic scenario?" I question.

"It's not about me, Layla. It's about what would be meaningful to Tyler."

"And you don't think Tyler wants the moment you two get engaged to be romantic?"

"I want it to be memorable for him. Are you going to fight me on this?" Caroline's doe eyes look up at me. It's hard to resist them as she begs me to help her create what she truly believes is going to be an epic proposal.

"No, I'm not going to fight you. I'm sorry. I just want to make sure that you have an experience that is so epic that your great-grandchildren are going to talk about it, and for the right reasons." I reach over and grasp Caroline's hand. "If you're lucky, you only get engaged once."

Caroline goes inside her head for a moment. When she reemerges, she brings her true feelings with her. "I'm worried that I've scared him. I mean, we're good. We've talked, but … We used to say things like '*when* we're married.' Lately he's been saying '*if* we get married.' I have to show him that my feelings haven't changed. I have to make him know that I'm just as invested as I was before I flaked."

"So you're planning a proposal you think a *guy* would like? Caroline, a proposal should be everything both of you wants to remember for the rest of your lives. It should encompass the things that you both find beautiful and meaningful. Paintball is something that Tyler enjoys, but he would never associate with you or your relationship."

Caroline lets out a hard breath and turns back to face the road. She flips through the little notebook she's been keeping her proposal ideas in and then rips out several pages.

"Well, I guess I'm back to square one." She looks sad and defeated. She wants so badly to prove to Tyler that she loves him.

"Hey. Just be present in your relationship with him and I promise that it's all going to work out exactly as it should. Now, let's just enjoy the scenic drive and catch up. I can't promise I won't talk non-stop about Natalie and Claire, but feel free to stop me if I begin to ramble on about them." I let a huge grin take over my face, which seems to help settle Caroline. I watch her physically relax as she leans back and pulls one knee to her chest.

I ask and Caroline is more than willing to tell me all about her European tour. I beam with excitement for her when she tells me more about taking the lead on Clooney's Lake Como home redesign, and that if that project wraps up in time she's hoping to get the Sting contract.

"These are real, actual words, Caroline. You just used the names Clooney and Sting in a sentence and neither was in reference to a dream you had!" We laugh at the awesomeness of it all and I remind her to take time and celebrate her success. She's so good at what she does and deserves every good thing that comes her way. I also make her promise to hire me as her personal assistant during both of those projects because there is no way I'm not going to take advantage of my best friend and get to meet George Clooney and Sting.

Caroline doesn't stop me when I tell her all about all the changes the twins are going through. They're growing so fast and it's hard to take sometimes. I have to remind myself not to blink because every time I do, I open my eyes to something new that they've learned how to do.

We talk like giddy girls about her one-day wedding and think that if she can hold off long enough, we really could get the twins to be flower girls. I can't promise they'll actually toss flower petals, but they'll look adorable toddling down the aisle with little satin baskets.

We pull onto the dirt road that leads to Rachel's and my heart starts to race with nervous excitement. I'm so glad Caroline and I had the conversation we did. It's going to make this moment even more spectacular.

"Oh my gosh! I've never seen a hot air balloon this close before!" Caroline exclaims. Rachel let Tyler use the only pink balloon they have because it's Caroline's favorite color. "Do you think she'll let me get a closer look? I don't want to intrude on whoever's plans."

"I'm sure it'll be fine," I tell her with a mischievous grin. She's really making this easy! We take a few steps away from the car when I remember the coat. "Oh! Caroline, hold on. You're going to need this." She looks at me with a quizzical expression but takes the coat anyway and puts it on. "Um … the balloon lets off weird air flows." It was the strangest excuse I had ever come up with off the cuff, but I was going to have to count on Caroline's ignorance to buy it.

We enter the house and find Rachel and Will leaning casually against the counters in the kitchen. I wonder how quickly they ran from the front door to their positions and chuckle.

"Hey babe!" Will says greeting me. "Thanks for coming all the way out here. I really appreciate it. There's no way we could get done what we need to if you hadn't brought what we needed."

"Absolutely!" I smile. "Rachel, this is Caroline. Caroline, this is Rachel."

"It's very nice to meet you," Rachel says.

"You, too. Um … I don't want to intrude on whoever is taking the balloon up, but would it be okay if I got a closer look? I've never seen a hot air balloon from this close before. Only seen them floating in the sky." Caroline is craning her neck to look through the doorway out through the windows in the sunroom for a better look at the balloon in the field of the backyard.

"Of course! This particular balloon is even more impressive up close." Rachel looks at me from the corner of her eyes and smiles at me knowingly.

Caroline walks through the sunroom with us close behind. As she steps onto the deck, she takes in the balloon in its enormity. She's entranced and it takes her a minute to see that there are two lines of pink and red rose petals forming a path to the balloon basket.

"Oh my gosh! This is beautiful!" She turns to Rachel who is already capturing every moment with her camera. "This is so romantic!"

"I was hoping you would think so," Tyler says as he rounds the corner of the house from where he had been hiding.

"Tyler?" Caroline is stunned and it takes her a moment to put everything together. She turns to me with a shocked face. "You!" She shakes her head in disbelief and then mouths the words "thank you" to me. I think the appreciation is for both talking her out of a tragic paintball proposal and for giving her a coat to cover her Barbie shirt. It was a cute shirt, but not what she would want captured for all eternity.

I smile as Will and I put our arms around each other proudly. After that, it takes Caroline approximately five seconds to start crying. Tyler meets her on the deck and takes her hand, leading her down the rose petal path to the basket. We can't hear exactly what Tyler is saying to Caroline, but from the practice rounds he had with Will I imagine he's saying something like "where you go, I go." He's telling her that he isn't going to let an ocean separate them. He's also telling her how much he loves her and that his life wouldn't be complete without her in it. And probably something about, "who would have known the day we met in Mrs. Kramer's English class freshman year that we would be here in this moment?"

When Tyler has poured his heart out to Caroline, he drops to one knee and pulls out the ring box that has been burning a hole in his pocket for weeks. He opens it and looks at Caroline and although we can't hear the words leave his mouth, I know he's saying what he has planned from Day One.

"Caroline, I love you. Be mine forever and marry me."

As expected, Caroline is speechless for the first time in her life. She covers her mouth and nods uncontrollably while tears of pure, unadulterated joy slide down her face. Tyler puts the ring on her finger, picking her up and kissing her as he stands.

I can't help the tear of my own joy for them both that escapes down my face. Will squeezes me closer to his side and kisses the top of my head as we watch Tyler help Caroline into the basket. Clive untethers the ropes and climbs in the basket behind them. Before we know it, we're waving to the happy couple as they rise into Carolina Blue sky.

The last few months have been filled with every emotion known to man. We went through so much with Michael. It seems redemptive that while Michael's life ended in this place, the new life Tyler and Caroline are embarking on would start here.

"We actually helped him pull this off," Will says to me. "Can you believe it?"

"Of course I can believe it. Everyone deserves a Happily Ever After, and this is the beginning of theirs."

THE END

Acknowledgements

Thank you so much to my amazing readers. You all fell in love with Will and Layla's story right from the beginning, and you have no idea what that means to me. Never I my wildest dreams did I ever imagine that this story would bring so much to you, make you feel so much. I feel forever bonded to you and you will always hold a special place in my heart.

Thank you to my Cone of Safety girls. You are my rocks in this crazy world we live in. Thank you for being there for me, being a sounding board, and for keeping it all in the Cone of Safety. I love you girls!

Thank you so much to the amazing team that astonishes me everyday as we work together in making my dreams come true. Rick Miles, you wonderfully snarky Englishman, I'm so grateful for your insight and vision. I am completely aware that I wouldn't be where I am without listening to your guidance and direction. And to my incredible agent, Italia Gandolfo, there are not enough words to tell you how appreciative I am of our partnership. I am on the most unbelievable adventure and I'm so happy to be arm in arm with you! You're the best mama bear ever!

Thank you to Marisa with Cover Me, Darling for creating a gorgeous cover. I love you for your vision and eternal patience with me! Thank you for being so awesome!

And to my wonderful husband and kids: I am so grateful to have you with me on this amazing journey. You are constantly encouraging me and excited for every new project that comes along. I'm so happy to share my life and all of this amazing joy with you!

Anchored: A Lake Series Novella

Also by AnnaLisa Grant:

The Lake Series:
The Lake
Troubled Waters
Safe Harbor

As I Am

FIVE

This book is a work of fiction. Names, characters, places, and incidents are either products of the author's imagination or are used fictitiously. Any resemblance to actual events or persons, living or dead, is entirely coincidental.

For more information, visit:
AnnaLisaGrant.com
Facebook.com/AuthorAnnalisaGrant

Cover art by Cover Me, Darling

CPSIA information can be obtained at www.ICGtesting.com
Printed in the USA
LVOW11s2102260916

506254LV00001B/191/P